The Wild Breed

Center Point Large Print

**This Large Print Book carries the
Seal of Approval of N.A.V.H.**

ॐ श्री गणेशाय नमः

CARTER TRAVIS YOUNG

The Wild Breed

CENTER POINT PUBLISHING

THORNDIKE, MAINE

To
My Mother and Father

This Center Point Large Print edition
is published in the year 2002 by arrangement with
Golden West Literary Agency.

Copyright ◉ 1960 by Carter Travis Young.

All rights reserved.

The text of this Large Print edition is unabridged.
In other aspects, this book may vary from the original edition.
Printed in Thailand. Set in 16-point Times New Roman type by
Bill Coskrey and Gary Socquet.

ISBN 1-58547-200-X

Library of Congress Cataloging-in-Publication Data.

Young, Carter Travis.
    The wild breed / Carter Travis Young.--Center Point large print ed.
    p. cm.
    ISBN 1-58547-200-X (lib. bdg. : alk. paper)
    1. Large type books. I. Title.

PS3575.O7 W49 2002
813'.54--dc21

2002067585

One

The train stood in the station, panting like a spent stallion. The dirty black plume of its smoke stretched beyond the eye's reach to the east, spreading in the distance to a shapeless smudge against the clean blue of the vast Texas sky.

Ben Webber stepped down stiffly from one of the yellow wooden cars. For a moment he stood unmoving on the platform, letting the noise and the excitement and the movement swirl around him, a tall, lean, gaunt figure in faded jeans, woolen shirt, and an old buckskin jacket bleached white by the sun. The clangor and the rhythmic swaying of the train were still with him in the way a rider, dismounting after a long day on the range, will still seem to feel his horse rolling against his thighs.

The train was a thing to make wonder break out in a man, Ben Webber thought, breathing deeply, but he was glad to be out of the stuffy car. Twenty-four hours of inhaling soot and dust and smoke, of bouncing and swaying to a motion that didn't allow you to adjust to it, tempered the awe you first felt for the train's beauty and its rushing speed. But now that the trip was over he didn't regret the quick decision to take the train. On horseback it would have taken three days or more of hard riding to reach Sweet Spring.

The urgency that had been in him since he read the news in Fort Worth two nights past stirred restlessly. Ben swung a pair of worn saddlebags over his left shoulder and started along the platform, cradling the Winchester in the crook of his right arm. A couple of waddies idly watching the train stared at him with open curiosity as he passed, noting the rifle, the bags, and the lean hips bare of a gun belt. Indifferent to their appraisal, Ben stepped down into the dusty street, letting his gaze roam ahead to take in the tall façade of the hotel, the frame buildings of general store, tobacconist, barber, drugstore, saddler, saloon, and bank. He walked forward with awkward, loping strides, the long line of his back stiff and straight.

Halfway along the street he saw a sign reading: ED MORGAN—GOOD EATS. Ben angled toward it, hunger tightening its hold in his empty belly. There was still a day's ride ahead of him and he hadn't had a hot meal since boarding the train.

He ate slowly and methodically, ignoring both the heat in the small restaurant and the buzz of conversation. In a surprisingly short time he had stowed away a thick slab of steak and a large helping of browned potatoes. The coffee was strong and hot, prompting Ben to pay Ed Morgan a silent tribute.

He glanced up to find the man behind the counter watching him approvingly.

"Stranger, ain't you?" Ed Morgan asked. He was a beefy man with very clean, soft hands, white like his apron.

Ben nodded.

"Come in on the train?"

"Yep."

"You figure on stayin' or jest passin' through?"

Ben didn't answer. He pushed his cup across the counter and Ed Morgan moved quickly to refill it.

"Not pryin' or anythin'," the restaurant owner said.

Ben nodded. He didn't resent the questions and he was not an uncivil man, but neither did he feel any desire or

6

need to talk. Two years alone on the ranch with only one Mexican rider who didn't speak much English had made a naturally silent disposition even more uncommunicative. Ben Webber was used to being alone and not talking for long periods. You might sing to cattle or even think out loud to a horse, but you didn't carry on a conversation.

Ed Morgan sighed. "Warm one today," he said hopefully.

Ben nodded again. All across the plain from Fort Worth he had seen the signs of an early spring, the near-desert prairie erupting in seas of gold and blue, the land under a warming sun wearing a fresh, clean, bright look like a woman putting on a party dress. Ben could remember a time when the coming of spring had brought a quickening to his blood, a keen response to the hope and the burgeoning life of a new season. But that was a long time ago when Ellen was still with him.

The thought of Ellen was a sharp reminder of the need to move on. He rose from the stool and bent to pick up his saddlebags and rifle.

"Good meal," he said as he went out, closing the door on Ed Morgan's look of surprise at the unexpected comment.

The livery stable was at the west end of town. It did not occur to Ben to ask anyone for directions. He was accustomed to doing things for himself. Like all of the buildings in Sweet Spring except the hotel, the stable was naked of paint. Whatever it might have seen had been scoured off by wind and rain. Even a casual eye saw loose boards that needed nailing, and Ben wondered how the roof had survived a severe winter. The observations were a lone rancher's habit, calling for no comment even to himself.

"Lookin' for someone, stranger?" The voice spoke

7

behind him, high-pitched and belligerent.

Ben pivoted easily. The voice belonged to a small, chunky man with a mass of curly, coal black hair and a pair of bright button eyes. "I'd like a horse," Ben said.

"Buyin' or rentin'?" The bright eyes weighed Ben's good but aged buckskin jacket, the worn jeans, the well-used boots that had been handmade of a soft, expensive leather—Ben's one extravagance.

"I'll be bringin' him back," Ben said.

"That's supposin' you get one," the little man said. His tone was suspicious. "I don't know you."

Ben regarded him calmly. He supposed that the man's size might account for his aggressiveness. It was something that seemed to run in small men who had to deal with Ben, as if they were trying to make up for having to look so high.

"Name's Ben Webber. I'll be ridin' to Red Peak. Happen to know how far it is?"

A different speculativeness shaded the button eyes. "Ten hours ride, maybe more." Abruptly he seemed to shed his suspicion for the new curiosity. "For some it's a lot longer comin' back. You must have a mighty good reason for goin' there."

"Good enough."

The little man grunted. Of a sudden he became all business. "Well, if you're goin' I can't stop you—but I've got just the horse you're looking for. You jest follow me."

He trotted briskly into the stable, Ben's easy strides keeping pace behind him. The horse turned out to be a big roan, clay red in color, deep-chested and powerful.

"I'm not a man to drive a hard bargain," the little man

said. "Dave Hennigan's my name, and any man in Sweet Spring will tell you I'm a fair man. I'm makin' you a real good price on this animal, and he's a fine one."

Ben waited. He liked the look of the roan, but as he'd expected Dave Hennigan's price for renting him was more than the animal was worth. "That's steep," Ben said.

"Not if you're goin' to Red Peak," Hennigan snapped. "You get five dollars back if I see you and him again. It ain't exactly a welcoming sort of town."

This was the second thinly veiled warning the little man had made about Red Peak. Ben shrugged, turning away to look over the other horses standing in the crude stalls. A door stood open at the end of the barn. Through it Ben could see the front wheels and board seat of a small rig. On impulse he walked across to the door and thoughtfully examined the wagon. There were signs of rust, but the wheels were solidly attached and the wagon was sturdy. One horse could pull it, Ben noted, but it wouldn't be the roan. One of the smaller, muscular, sure-footed mustangs he now saw in the corral behind the stable would handle himself better pulling the rig over rough ground.

He swung back to Dave Hennigan, who had followed him to the doorway. "Suppose I might rent a rig like this in Red Peak when I'm headin' back this way?"

"Doubt it," the little man snapped quickly. "And if you want this one you'll have to pay good for it. Maybe you figure on comin' back, but a man can't count on much these days."

Ben let him talk. He had already made up his mind. He would need the wagon for the return trip, and it was true that there might not be one available where he was going.

Hennigan's figure was high for the rig, but he didn't value one of the mustangs as much as the roan. Ben offered him ten dollars less than he asked.

"I can't do it," Dave Hennigan complained. "Hell, I don't even know what you're plannin' on usin' it for. You won't find a wagon like this everywhere, I tell you. I couldn't afford to let you have it for less." His bright gaze grew more intent. "What *do* you figure on doin' with the wagon? Seems kind of funny, haulin' it all that way. You bringin' somethin' back? I got a right to know, it bein' my rig and all."

Ben's blue eyes were expressionless, but the lines in his face seemed to deepen as if with a freshly remembered grief. He regarded the smaller man thoughtfully, weighing his claim to an answer.

Ben's words came out blunt and unemotional. "I'm bringin' back my son."

Startled, Dave Hennigan stared at him. "Your boy?" His glance flicked from the wagon back to Ben, who could read the question growing in the little man's face.

"He's dead," Ben said.

"Well, now. Dead," Dave Hennigan murmured. "Now I'm mighty sorry to hear that. It ain't a nice thing to see your own flesh-and-blood go before you. No sirree." He hesitated, fighting a brief private battle of his own. At length he spoke reluctantly. "In that case I reckon you might have it for your price. I don't aim to be a hard man, Mr. Webber."

Ben could see the brightness growing behind his eyes as his quick mind switched again and the curiosity became more avid. The button eyes swiveled in the dark face to take in Ben's naked hip. Dave Hennigan jerked his head toward it meaningfully.

"You don't look like no gunman, and I suppose you know what you're doin', but do you figure on maybe somethin' else besides jest bringin' back your boy? Like maybe findin' out who killed him? Don't know as I'd care to rent the rig if you was gunnin' for somebody in Red Peak."

Ben's reply was laconic. He looked suddenly older. "He wasn't shot. He was hanged."

Two

Ben camped out that night on a ledge overlooking a broad table of barren land, bony with ridges and shot with the veins of endless gullies, peopled with mesquite bushes and an occasional family of gnarled, stubby oaks. It was useless land, Ben thought. The soil would yield little to the plow, and cattle would lose themselves in the narrow ravines. Beyond the table to the west swelled a ring of hills some fifty miles away. The setting sun had reflected red off a massive fist of rock striking up to meet the sky. That would be Red Peak.

The wind that had picked up in the late afternoon held into the night, sweeping unimpeded across the great plain, bringing a penetrating cold that made Ben huddle close to the fire, arms clamped against his sides for warmth. He ate a meal of jerked beef, hard bread and coffee. Afterward he held callused hands out to the flames to warm them before trying to roll a cigarette. The cold bit deep, as if it were not all outside but had found a core of coldness inside him. The years took away the fire that had once burned high and warm in a man.

Ben thought of Dave Hennigan's question. It had not surprised him. There would be others who would wonder at his coming and there might be trouble. It wouldn't be easy to explain how it was that he felt no harsh thrust of anger, no rage of sorrow. Time wore away the edges of grief, too, until it was no longer an arrow of pain but had become a dull ache you'd carried with you so long that sometimes you could almost forget it was there.

He thought of Ellen. It was easier to let his mind remember her after two years. And the funny thing was that now he always pictured her as she was in the beginning, in the good years when she was young and spirited and gay, her body soft and warm and eager with love. He could see her in the one big room of the timber house, the way it was before he put on the addition after Jethroe was born. Her hair was a shiny black like a crow's wing. That and her eyes, gray with flecks of green in them, showed the Irish that was in her. She was slim and small against Ben, but there was a surprising strength in her when she fought him, playing at resistance, laughing with the joy that was never far beneath the surface with her, her eyes sparkling with challenge, until that sudden moment would come to both of them and the laughter would die and the slim strong arms would tighten around his neck.

The years were never easy. Ben had had to fight to scrape a bare living out of the small ranch, fighting blizzard and snow of winter, heat and drought of summer, the attrition of sickness and rustler and weather always cutting into his small herd of cattle. But there was his stubborn pride to keep him going, and there was Ellen, and then there was Jethroe.

Memory came up abruptly against the bitter knowledge of what Jet Webber had become. They had spoiled him, he and Ellen, putting themselves as a protective barrier between the boy and hardship or want, indulging the wildness in him, letting it grow free until he became a youth who reminded you of a wild horse that's never known rope or bit or the weight of a man on his back, who knows only his own need and temper, who will fight as if the devil is inside him. And for a time they laughed at the untrammeled spirit of the boy, even taking a little pride in it, not seeing the vanity and the selfishness and the cruel temper until it was too late.

Ben should have known. He had even taught the boy to handle a gun before he was fifteen, giving in to the persistent pleas. When Jet would sneak off for hours while Ben worked alone on chores the boy should have been learning, Ben let it go, knowing from the distant crack and echo that Jet was practicing over and over again with the Colt that seemed so much too long and too heavy for the youthful willow of his body.

For his sixteenth birthday Ben gave him his own new gun. Seeing the glitter in Jet's eyes, the man's way he tied the holster to his thigh, hanging low, Ben thought to take him down a peg. Half amused, half serious, he shook the bullets from his own gun, bade Jet do the same, and challenged him. Ben's gun never got clear of its holster before he found himself staring down the shiny new barrel of Jet's gun.

And the boy was laughing at him in a way that had no fun in it but something of contempt.

That was the first time Ben saw the fear in Ellen's eyes.

During the next year he saw it many times. That was the year, too, when she first started to cough so much. He saw her getting thinner and attributed it to the worry and the nights when she couldn't sleep because Jet wasn't home and might be in trouble.

It was late that summer when Tim Hogan rode over from his neighboring ranch to talk to Ben about Jet. The men in the territory were getting tired of the way Jet swaggered around town, taunting grown men, letting them see the snake-fast dart of his gun hand. If Ben didn't put a stop to it, Hogan declared, some of the other men would. Stung to anger by the truth in Hogan's warning, Ben told him to mind his own business. Ben could take care of his own boy without help.

Ben had never cared much for Tim Hogan, but he got along with him as he did with most men. Hogan was a heavy drinker, given to meanness when he was drunk. More than once Ben had seen Nell Hogan with bruises showing on her face and arms after Tim had been to town drinking. Still there had been no call for what had happened.

As a young man Ben himself had known what it was to fight and kill—against the Indian, the Confederate soldier, the outlaw gun. But if he had killed it was because he had to, not because he was out to prove his toughness. If there had been wildness in him that once led to—

Angrily Ben jerked away from the thought. Hunched under the ground blanket by the dying fire, he tried to dam the flood of painful memory. It was no use. The torrent spilled through, too strong to be contained.

Ben was not in town that September night. Jet, openly

scornful of his father's warning about staying out of trouble, had ridden into town late in the afternoon. What started the trouble with Tim Hogan Ben was never able to find out, except that Tim was drunk and his tongue was loose. The inquiry was never pushed too far because the law called it a fair duel.

That wasn't the way Ben saw it. You had to take it into account when a man was drunk. Hogan was hardly responsible for the words which lashed Jet to killing anger. What's more, you didn't draw on a man when you knew he was no match for you, unless you were forced into it. Hogan carried a gun, like most men, and he knew how to use it, but he was no gunslinger, and in his drink-dulled state he was certainly no match for Jet's cold and sober talent with his gun hand.

The boy drew on him. While Hogan clawed clumsily at his holster Jet shot him twice in the chest.

He came home that night alone, saying nothing of what had happened. The sheriff arrived about an hour later, and Jet came out of his room to listen to what the sheriff said to Ben, looking on with his face as cool and calm as if he'd been caught in a schoolboy's prank.

When the sheriff left, Ben turned on Jet, sick with anger and guilt. He saw the arrogance in the young-old face, the insolent smile and the indifferent shrug, and he thought of Nell Hogan. Fury drove the fist that smashed into Jet's mouth, sending him reeling backward to tumble over a chair and crash to the floor. Ellen screamed, and the boy's hand slashed down toward his hip. Ben stepped in fast, the toe of his boot slamming viciously into Jet's wrist, forcing a cry of pain. Ben slid the gun from Jet's holster and threw it across the room.

"You've done enough killing for one night!" he raged.

"I wasn't going to—"

"Why not? That's the way you fight, ain't it? It wouldn't matter to you that I'm not carryin' a gun—or that I'm your father!"

"He had a gun!" Jet cried.

"But he didn't know how to draw it, did he? You had everything your way. He was even drunk, blind drunk or I'm damned. You couldn't lose!"

"You didn't hear what he said!"

"Was it so bad? Was it so bad you had to kill him?"

"He had his chance!"

"You lie!" Ben reached to grab a fistful of Jet's shirt, dragging him to his feet. "If he'd had a chance you never would have tried to draw on him!"

Jet's face went white. "Don't say that," he cried, his voice trembling. "You hear me, don't say that!"

"Ben, please!" Ellen tried to come between them and he brushed her away. "Ben, don't!"

"I'm going to whip him," Ben said harshly. "I'm going to whip him the way I should have a long time ago. And then I'm going over to Nell Hogan and beg her forgiveness. You hear that, boy? I'm going to beg her. I'll tell her that my boy is some kind of a snake with poison in him, only I didn't know it. You want to try for your gun, boy? It's over there. But you'll have to move fast because I'm not drunk the way Tim Hogan was."

But Jet didn't move. White-faced, he stood there, and an uncontrollable rage overpowered Ben, rage born of the anguish that was so strong it sickened him. Ben hit him.

The boy got up and came at him, fists swinging. Ben knocked him down again. Ellen cried and tried to stop them, but nothing would have turned Ben aside at that moment. The boy kept getting up until his face was a smear of blood, and after a while he was bent over in an odd way from a blow to the chest. At last he went down again and he couldn't get up. Ben stood over him. The haze began to clear from his brain and he heard Jet sobbing, heard the chilling words. "You ever touch me again and I'll kill you! You hear?" Jet choked. "I'll kill you!"

In the morning he was gone. They never saw him again. In the five years since that night of anger many rumors and stories about Jet had reached Ben. Maybe he had been too ready to believe them, remembering Jet's callous indifference to the fact of killing a man, recalling the threat of those final words. Yet the proof of those whispers that told of gambling and robbing and killing seemed to lie in the news that reached Ben in Fort Worth just two days ago, the knowledge that Jet had been hanged for another murder.

This was the thing Ellen had feared, and in a way Ben could be glad that she had not lived to know the added pain. For in her the grief of Jet's leaving, and the manner of it, had never abated. It was always there in the open with her, like a wound that refused to heal. It seemed to Ben that she began to fade, to lose the spark of life, from the time Jet left. The tuberculosis grew and spread in her until at the last it seemed that she was only a frail and feeble cough, becoming weaker, thinner, paler.

He buried her on a knoll within sight of the timber house, three years from the time Jet left home, two years before he felt the inevitable rope.

Now Ben was coming to bring the boy home that he might be buried beside his mother. It seemed a simple, necessary thing to him, something Ellen would have wanted, something he must do. Then everything would be complete like a story ended.

Ben lay still on the ledge above the wind-swept table of land. The rush of memory had spent itself. His mind seemed empty, drained of both bitterness and hope. He shivered. The fire beside which he lay had died to a pile of gray ash that gleamed red underneath in the stirring of the wind but no longer gave any warmth.

It was the same with a man, Ben mused, returning to the thought. There came a time when there was no flame left, no heat, only ashes that glowed feebly. Like a dying fire, or like October of the year. No real grief any more, no hot anger, no thirst for revenge, no spring or summer. The useful, productive days were all behind. For some men this time came late, for others early, as it had come to Ben at forty-two. Alone now, he had spent the days that mattered, and only the winter lay ahead. There was no one to whom he could leave anything of himself—not even his name.

Ben Webber lay on the hard ground, thinking of these things without self-pity but simply as the way of life. He listened to the wind prodding the mesquite into crackling motion and whining in the gullies, and he felt the cold deep inside him. Reluctantly he left the cover of his blanket for a moment to draw fresh wood over to the fire. Sparks flared. As he drifted toward sleep new flames licked at the dry branches.

Three

Sheriff Jake Howell was a big, surly-looking man with an unexpected heartiness of manner. A heavy black beard and puffy lower eyelids that narrowed his eyes gave the mean cast to his face, but he had a way of talking that was like the tone a humorless man will adopt when talking to children, maybe a little too loud and too friendly seeming. Ben noted that he also tended to put words into your mouth that you hadn't said.

"I'm sure glad you came straight to see me, Mr. Webber," Howell said. "It was the right thing to do. There's sure no point in rootin' for trouble when there's no cause, less'n you know all the facts."

"I don't aim to be causin' any trouble, Sheriff," Ben said quietly.

He had been riding into a late afternoon sun when he reached Red Peak, a cluster of frame buildings huddled together within the long shadow of a massive fist of red rock. The town was at the west end of the broad table of land above which he had camped the night before. It had a bleak, unfriendly look. There were houses grouped close to each other at the south end of town, as if for protection. There was a two-story hotel and a saloon that matched its height, and around these two main buildings were the usual shops and stores and offices. Ben had come directly to the sheriff's office, tethering the mustang with the rig outside.

"'Course not," Howell said, swinging away to stare through a dirt-stained window at the wagon. He had a habit of turning in his wooden swivel chair when he talked, so that he wasn't looking at you when the words came. "But it would be only human if you felt your boy was wronged and wanted to find the folks who did it. Blood's thick, Mr. Webber, there's no denyin' that, and I'm not blamin' you for feelin' the way you do."

"I just want to find out what happened."

"Understand now, Mr. Webber," Howell said quickly, "I wasn't involved. As soon as I found out what Jet Webber done, I deputized a couple of the boys and went lookin' for him. I knew there'd be trouble if I didn't find him first, the way feelin's was runnin' high in town."

"Just what did Jet do?" Ben asked patiently.

"Now don't you go gettin' riled," the sheriff said aggrievedly. "I understand how you feel and all, but Jet was too quick with a gun and that's the truth of it. There's no use sayin' different."

"You didn't find him," Ben prodded, "you and your deputies?"

"Well, no." Howell swiveled away in the chair, not meeting Ben's eyes. "Ross Pardee was a man well liked in this town. When Jet Webber killed him, some of the men felt pretty strong about it. From what I was told, there was a crowd of 'em and they kind of got carried away, the way men will. They found the boy before I did."

"You talked to the men who did it?"

"Well, no, I couldn't find anybody who'd admit bein' in on the lynching party, but that's natural, Mr. Webber. Me and my deputies wasn't even in town when it happened. Folks kind of took the law into their own hands, and they wasn't anxious to tell me they were the ones that did it."

"You mean there was no trial?" Ben asked sharply.

"Now don't you be gettin' excited," Howell said quickly. "Maybe the people in town acted too hasty, but your Jet would have been hanged anyway, Mr. Webber. It don't much matter, a day or two sooner or later."

"It matters that a man has to be proved guilty," Ben said, for the first time wondering if there was something more back of Jake Howell's uneasiness than he yet knew.

"Now wait right there," Howell said nervously. "You jest hold on a minute now, Mr. Webber. There's no question about Jet bein' guilty. There's no question about that at all. If you knew all the facts you wouldn't be hintin' that some injustice was done. It wasn't like that at all."

"Suppose you tell me just how it was," Ben said.

Howell swung to stare out the window. "First off, you got to understand how things are in Red Peak," he said, lowering his voice as if he were afraid of being overheard. "There's been trouble before between John Matson and some of the smaller ranchers here."

"Who's Matson?"

"Owns the saloon. You probably saw it ridin' in. The Gold Nugget. He's lent some of the ranchers money when they were in trouble, Ross Pardee bein' one of them. When Ross couldn't pay, Matson was figurin' to foreclose on him. Your boy Jet was one of Matson's hired hands." The sheriff shifted his bulk uncomfortably in the swivel chair. "When trouble started threatenin', Matson hired some men who are fast with a gun. Folks didn't take too much to that."

"There was trouble between Pardee and Matson?"

"Well, it was brewin'. Ross kind of figured that Matson pulled a fast one, and maybe he did at that. But it was all fair and legal," the sheriff added hastily. "Ross owed the money and Matson had a right to collect when it was due, or he got the Pardee ranch."

Ben regarded him thoughtfully. The picture was becoming clearer now. "Where did Jet figure in this?" he asked.

"He killed Pardee," Howell said. "Oh, there's no doubt he done it, Mr. Webber. He was seen. He didn't know it, but there was a witness. No one knows for sure jest exactly why he done it, or what happened between the two of them before the shootin', but Jet Webber shot Pardee."

"But if the man was lookin' for trouble—"

"Ross Pardee was no gunman, Mr. Webber. And Jet never even give him a chance to draw. A man's entitled to fair warning, and your boy didn't give it."

Ben's face felt wooden. The sheriff's words told him what he had feared, confirming the worst he had ever been led to believe about the bad streak in Jet.

"That's why feelin's run so high in town," Howell said. "Folks around here figure a man who kills in cold blood ought to pay for it. I know that's hard for you to under-stand, him bein' your son and all, but I can't say as I blame the men for doin' what they did. It's like I say, Mr. Webber, if I'd caught him he'd have hanged jest the same."

Ben didn't want to hear any more. Though he'd been pre-pared for it, the truth about Jet still hit hard. "I'd like to talk to the man who saw him do it," he said tonelessly. "I'm not doubtin' your word, Sheriff. I just have to hear it for myself."

For a moment the sheriff was silent. He didn't look at Ben. "I'm sorry, Mr. Webber, I can't have you doin' that. Like I been telling you, I know how you feel. If it was my son I'd likely have come here jest the way you did, huntin' for the ones who strung him up. But I don't want no more trouble here and that's the size of it. You take my advice, Mr. Webber, and you ride on back home. Gettin' revenge on people who acted hasty, maybe, without thinkin', but feelin' they was doin' the right thing, ain't gonna change things none."

"I didn't come for that," Ben said. He was thinking that the sheriff didn't really listen to what a man said.

Howell swiveled to face him. His eyes were watchful behind the puffy lids. "Jest what did you come here for, Mr. Webber?"

"I aim to take Jet home for buryin'," Ben said quietly. "His mother would have wanted it that way."

Howell's bearded face was slack with surprise. "You come all this way for that? That's why you brought a wagon?"

"Yep."

The surprise came under control. Howell's eyes narrowed with quick suspicion. He swung away from Ben in the swivel chair. "I'm sorry, Mr. Webber. I can't let you do that."

It was Ben's turn to be surprised. "Why not?" he asked, his voice sharp.

"I told you I don't want no more trouble here," Howell said angrily. "I appreciate your feelings, but the boy's been buried and that's the end of it. You try to dig him up now and you'll jest be stirrin' things up."

Ben controlled his own rise of feeling. "It's little enough to ask," he said, tight-reining his voice.

"It's agin the law! I can't allow it." The sheriff glared at him. "What's done is done. I give you more than your son give, Mr. Webber—fair warning. Let things be!"

Ben's eyes, blue and cold, held the sheriff's steadily. There was something here he didn't understand. Howell's nervousness, his sudden anger, had deeper roots than Ben had uncovered.

He rose stiffly. "I came here to get Jet's body and take him home," he said, the words stubborn with purpose. "That's my right and I don't know of any law that can deny it to me. I'm not leavin' without him!"

He left the sheriff staring after him, his face flushed red under the dark beard.

The livery stable was at the north end of town where the main street ended and foothills began. Here an occasional cottonwood gave shade from the sun. In the distance where the hills climbed steeply there were signs of greenery, dark patches against the slopes that hinted at tall, rich grasses and fertile hidden valleys where cattle could grow fat and sleek.

Ben left his horse and rig, making sure the mustang would be well cared for. The animal had proved sturdy and nimble on his feet in the rough country. In their brief journey a communion had come to exist between the man and the horse, Ben's hands gently urging on the reins, the animal quickly responsive. Ben wanted him for the trip back, wanted him well fed and rested and brushed down.

As he left the stable Ben saw a man watching him from a distance, standing next to a small frame building with a wooden cross mounted at the peak of its gabled roof. It appeared that he had been working in a small garden laid out in neat rows in the shadow of the church, which stood alone on the fringes of the town east of the livery stable. Ben reckoned that a town as rough as Red Peak was supposed to be wouldn't take much to churchgoing. But a preacher would come in handy for burying where men died young and fast—like Ross Pardee and Jethroe Webber.

The preacher seemed eager to leave his work as Ben approached. Close to, the garden didn't look as promising as it had at a distance. It was neat, like the man who laid it out, but it wasn't hoed deep enough. Neither the preacher's clothes nor the man beneath them looked as if they were made for hard work. But clothes and looks could fool you, Ben thought. A man who would come here and try to preach and keep his church going had a strength somewhere inside him.

"Good day, sir," the man called as Ben came up to him. "You're a stranger in these parts, if I'm not mistaken."

"I am," Ben said.

"Then welcome to you, sir." He held out his hand. "I'm the Reverend Templeton."

Ben took his hand, briefly studying the man. He had the precise way of talking of an educated man, and he had a prominent Adam's apple that kept bobbing up and down in his throat as if apologizing. A preacher shouldn't be so nervous.

"I'm Ben Webber."

The slender hand withdrew hastily. "Webber? Do you bear any relationship to the young man who—who—?"

"He was my son."

"I see." The lump moved nervously in the thin neck. "My sympathies to you, Mr. Webber."

"I thank you, Reverend." Ben hesitated. "It was my son I come to see you about."

"I'm afraid I—I can tell you very little about him. He was not a member of my church, of course." The careful words had lost their friendliness.

"I come to take my son home, Mr. Templeton, to bury him beside his mother there. I figured that, seein' as you might have officiated at the buryin' here, you might be able to help me some."

The preacher drew himself up stiffly like a soldier at attention. "I'm afraid you are under some misapprehension, sir. I can assure you that I had nothing to do with, ah, any services in connection with your son."

Ben frowned. "I take it you're the only preacher here."

"That is quite right, Mr. Webber. But you must understand that, even if I had been called upon to do so, I could not have performed a Christian service for your son."

For a moment Ben regarded him in silence. "That takes some understanding, Mr. Templeton," he said at last.

"I'm sorry to have to say this, Mr. Webber," the preacher said. "You seem like a God-fearing man. But your son was a paid gunman and a murderer. He had renounced all claim to God's mercy."

For a moment anger shook Ben. He had to struggle to keep from putting his hands on the slender figure before him. "Can you be so sure in speaking for God?" he demanded harshly.

Mr. Templeton took a step back, his lump bobbing rapidly in his throat. "I must judge things as I see them, Mr.

Webber. The people of my flock would not think it right if a murderer should be buried among their kin with God's blessing."

Ben's anger left him as quickly as it had come. He stared intently at the preacher, feeling an uneasy stirring of memory, seeing in this righteous man something of his own uncompromising hardness toward Jet five years before.

"I won't be botherin' you more, Mr. Templeton," Ben said heavily, "if you'll be good enough to tell me if you know where my son was buried."

"I'm afraid I can't help you, sir," the preacher said coldly. "It was done at night after the hanging. I've heard that some of Mr. Matson's men, er, cut him down." He spoke Matson's name with distaste. "But I had nothing to do with it and could not name those who did."

"You'll at least be knowing where the cemetery is, I suppose?"

"Of course." The preacher's mouth got a pinched look in reaction to Ben's sarcasm. "You'll find it on the far side of that hill just to the north of here. But I'm afraid that is all I can tell you."

"Would there be anybody who might know more than you, Mr. Templeton?" A thought came suddenly to Ben as he spoke. "Might there have been a coffin made?"

"Well, I—I'm sure there was. That would be Luke Harris. He makes all the—ah—coffins."

Ben felt a dislike for this careful-speaking man of God. A reverend should not be so fearful of the words of death. "I thank you, Mr. Templeton," he said abruptly, turning away.

"Mr. Webber! I hope you didn't come to Red Peak in a spirit of, ah, revenge. Surely you must see that more killing will not bring your son back. There has been trouble enough already—"

"I'm obliged to you for the advice," Ben interrupted him testily. "But I told you why I came."

As he turned his back on the man he wondered at the anger that was in him, so ready to hurl its thunder. He had believed such storms of feeling to have long since blown away.

It was sunset when he walked back through the town. The street and its buildings were already in shadow, but the crest of Red Peak still stood in the full blaze of the sun, glowing red like a branding iron. He found Luke Harris putting away his tools behind the hotel, where he was working on an extension.

"Yep, I be the same," the carpenter said. "Luke Harris, that's me.

"Might you be the one makes coffins?"

Harris thoughtfully spat a stream of tobacco juice in the general direction of a long-legged spider that scuttled fast along the ground to escape the brown torrent. "Might be," he said. "Build just about everything that's made of wood around these parts."

"Maybe you'll remember makin' one for a man named Jethroe Webber."

Harris's large yellow eyes examined Ben. "Never knew his name was Jethroe," he said. "Jet, he was called around here. Why might you be askin'?"

"Name's Ben Webber. Jet's father."

Harris nodded. "Don't look much like him, that's sure." His eyes went to Ben's hip. "Never saw Jet Webber without a gun, neither."

"You made his coffin?"

"Yep. That is, I had one on hand already made and they come and took it. John Matson paid for it afterwards." He peered at Ben through those open, yellow eyes that didn't reveal much of what went on behind them. "The boy worked for Matson. I reckon you knew that."

"I did." Ben watched the carpenter closely. "Would you know where he was buried?"

"Nope." Harris looked away, staring up at the flaming mass of rock towering behind the hotel. "They come for the box, that's all I know."

"Who?"

Harris stirred uneasily, shifting his feet. "Couple of friends of his, I suppose. Don't just remember who they was."

And Ben Webber knew with sudden intuition that Harris was lying. There seemed to be no reason for it, but there it was. He thought of the sheriff's evasions and the preacher's hostility. An undefined suspicion quickened in him.

"You had a busy time," he said.

Harris looked startled. "What's that mean?"

"You had a call for two coffins."

"Oh. You'll be meanin' Ross Pardee. He wasn't buried until Monday. I made one special for him."

"Would you know where he was buried?"

"Well, now, I wasn't there, but the preacher, Mr. Templeton, he could tell you. Miss Nancy arranged things with him."

"Miss Nancy?"

"That's Ross Pardee's sister." Harris's yellow eyes met Ben's again. "You're a mighty curious man, Mr. Webber."

"My son was hanged, Mr. Harris."

The carpenter spat some tobacco juice, not aiming at anything this time. "He was a killer, Mr. Webber. Round here folks don't cotton to a gunslinger who'll shoot a man down without givin' him a fair chance."

Ben felt weary of explaining. "I've no quarrel with that," he said, "if a man's guilty. All I've come for is my son's body."

"You expect folks to believe that?"

"I don't rightly care," Ben said. "But I'd be grateful if you'd answer me one question."

Harris chewed his tobacco noncommittally. "I might."

"Why would you be lying to me, Mr. Harris?"

The chewing stopped. Harris stooped toward the nest of tools on the ground beside him. When he straightened there was an ax in his hand. His yellow eyes were baleful. "For a man who don't tote a gun, Mr. Webber," he said, "you're mighty loose with words."

Ben looked without expression at the ax balanced in the carpenter's gnarled hands. "Everyone I've talked to in this town is mighty free with words, Mr. Harris, until I ask about my son. It makes a man think there might be a reason."

The lanky man spat deliberately at Ben's feet. "I wouldn't push it, Mr. Webber. That's my last word to you. Folks don't take to a stranger pryin' and tryin' to stir up trouble over somethin' that's done."

"Done and buried?" Ben asked with an edge to his voice.

Harris colored under the dark leather of his skin. "I wouldn't want to have to make you a coffin, Mr. Webber."

But he said it as if he didn't find the thought displeasing. For a moment longer Ben held his gaze on the man's face, wondering at the malice he found there. Then he turned away, the movement slow and easy. He saw Luke Harris's shoulders begin to relax, the heavy weight of the ax blade dipping. Ben pivoted and stepped in to him fast, his right hand reaching to catch the ax handle as Harris brought it up. Ben jerked the ax straight out from the man's body. Harris's grip held and Ben's movement pulled his arm taut. Ben brought up his leg and slammed the carpenter's stiff arm down against his thigh in the way a man will break wood across his knee. With a grunt of pain Harris dropped the ax. Ben stepped back. His fist lashed out and landed solid against the carpenter's jaw. Harris went down.

Stunned, Harris lay sprawled on the ground, shaking his head. Ben waited for the yellow eyes to focus on him.

"I don't take kindly to threats," Ben said.

He left the man on the ground, clutching his arm and moaning to himself.

Five

The fat woman behind the counter in the hotel gave Ben a queer look when she heard his name, and she asked for payment of a day's rent in advance. Ben reckoned the whole town knew he was there by now. There was no welcome in the woman's face.

From the window of his second-floor room he watched

darkness close down on Red Peak. Noise seemed to rise with the coming of night. Unseen hooves thudded loud on the dirt street. Boots clumped along the board sidewalk. From somewhere up the street there came a peal of woman's laughter and a man's hoarse guffaw.

Ben thought about the unfriendliness he'd met in Red Peak. That he might have expected. He was a stranger and the father of a man the town had hated enough to hang without a trial. But the evasiveness was a different thing, without explanation that he could find satisfactory. Perhaps there was guilt behind it, a town's uneasiness over a deed of violence, one they wanted to forget the way a man will seek to hide a thing he's ashamed of. Ben's presence was a reminder. But even that explanation didn't seem to account for the apparent opposition to his taking Jet's body home for burial.

One man might give him an answer and tell him where Jet was put to rest, the man whose name kept cropping up wherever Ben probed—John Matson.

The Gold Nugget was a fancier place than Ben expected and bigger than a town the size of Red Peak seemed to justify, with red plush curtains over the windows and a carpet on the floor instead of sawdust. There was a long bar of polished mahogany. Behind it in an ornate gold-colored frame was a painting of a woman big as life lying on red velvet cushions, a woman plumper and softer and pinker than any had a right to be. Toward the front of the room two large faro tables were crowded with players and watchers. At smaller tables some men drank and others played at cards, their eyes intent and their faces grim the way all men seem to get when they gamble. Several women with rouged cheeks moved among the tables or watched the games, flirting with the men. Their handsomeness surprised Ben. One, a slip of a girl with bare shoulders and a figure as plump-chested as that of the woman in the painting, only slimmer through the rest of her, was even prettier than the women in the music hall at Fort Worth.

Ben ordered whisky at the bar. He noted a redheaded barrel of a man with his holster tied low against his thigh watching him through eyes as cold and unblinking as a snake's. There had been others like him along the boardwalk, leaning against hitching posts or holding up the walls of buildings, quiet men whose faces were insolent with challenge, who wore the stamp of gunmen like a brand. Hired guns. And Jet had been one like them. The knowledge brought a momentary sickness to Ben's belly and his eyes were hot. He threw back his head and downed the harsh whisky in a gulp. What did it matter how the town reacted to his coming? Nothing could change the fact of what Jet had been.

"Let me buy you another," a voice spoke close to his ear.

Ben turned his head. "I've no objection," he said easily. "But a man likes to know who he's drinkin' with."

"John Matson, Mr. Webber. Welcome to my place."

Matson motioned to the bartender, who started to pour two glasses from the bottle he'd used before. Matson checked him with a gesture. The bartender pulled a different bottle from under the bar. It was still corked and full.

"News travels fast in Red Peak," Ben said.

Matson smiled in a friendly way, showing strong white teeth as if he were proud of them. "Jake Howell does a lot of talking," he said.

"I noticed that."

"I seen Luke Harris talkin' to the sheriff," Matson said. "Luke looked like he wasn't feelin' very good."

Ben said nothing. He took a sip of the whisky the bartender had poured. It was a lot smoother than the other.

"Too bad about his arm," Matson said. "Luke's the only good carpenter in town."

Ben eyed him levelly. "A friend of yours?"

The other man laughed outright. "He'll recover. Besides, I never was a man to interfere in a private disagreement."

Ben nodded. Matson had a smooth way of talking. He was a handsome man, not much younger than Ben, yet Ben had the feeling that he himself looked a great deal older. Matson had deep sideburns and long wavy hair, a silver gray where it was brushed past his ears. Bill Cody had the same long hair, Ben remembered, and the same full mustache. Somehow the gray seemed to add to Matson's good looks, without aging him, in contrast to the way the harsh iron gray of Ben's own close-cropped hair seemed to serve as a sign of encroaching age.

There was a difference in their clothes, too. Ben's were worn and colorless. Matson's clothes were new and expensive and resplendent with color. He wore a checked vest over a red shirt. His pants were a shiny black. Everywhere you looked he seemed to wink with reflected light—from the gold of his watch chain across his middle, from the heavy silver buckle of his gun belt, from the silver plating on his ivory-butted gun, from silver spurs attached to his soft black boots.

"Jet Webber worked for me," Matson said. "I reckon you

know that. I needn't tell you how I feel about what happened to him."

"How do you feel, Mr. Matson?"

For a moment the man's brown eyes were as shining hard as the polished mahogany of the bar. "He was one of my boys. I don't know just what happened between him and Pardee the time of the shooting, but Jet wasn't the kind of man to draw on another man without giving warning the way they say he did. Your Jet was fast, Mr. Webber, right fast. He'd no need to dry-gulch a man even if he'd a mind to. I know he was seen to do it, but still I believe he had a right to a hearing. Those who lynched him haven't heard the last of what happened from me, Mr. Webber. I haven't been able to learn the names of those who were so quick with a rope, but I will. Hangin' Jet was a way of gettin' back at me, too, and I'm not forgettin' that. I'm not a man who forgets either a good turn or a bad one."

He tossed down his drink, reached for the bottle and poured both his own and Ben's glass full. Ben left the glass there on the bar. He was thinking that Matson's words sounded mighty fine while he was talking, but when he stopped you weren't just sure what he had said.

"Just what was Jet hired to do for you, Mr. Matson?" Ben asked thoughtfully.

Matson leaned back against the bar, hooking his elbows over the edge, letting his eyes rove over the room. Ben followed his look and noticed the pretty girl with the bare shoulders watching them. She smiled as Matson's gaze came to her.

"You have a right to know the way things stand here," Matson said. "A lot of the small ranchers around here don't like the size of my land holdings. A small man will always resent a big one, Mr. Webber. I've bought up land that was available, land anyone could have bought if he had the money. This is rugged country and it isn't easy for a cow-puncher to make a livin' off it. Some who couldn't keep goin' have hated me because I could." He shrugged as if to indicate that he didn't care what men thought of him. "I've tried to help my neighbors. I've even lent money to some who came to me for it, lent it on the land, Mr. Webber, all fair and legal. When they couldn't pay me back I've been forced to take over the land sometimes, if I could see they weren't going to be able to work things out. Maybe that sounds hard to you, but I'm a businessman, Mr. Webber. I pay my debts and I expect others to do the same."

"That doesn't tell me why you hired gunmen," Ben said.

"You've been listening to loose talk about me," Matson said, anger roughening his voice. "But there's two sides to anything. Sure, I hired me some men who could take care of themselves with a gun. Jet Webber was one of them. I've had to deal with troublemakers, those who didn't like havin' to pay their debts when they was due. I'm a man who doesn't shy away from trouble, Mr. Webber, if it comes at me."

Ben said nothing. Matson seemed fond of telling you what kind of man he was, and Ben knew you could seldom take such a man at his own spoken estimate of himself. But Ben had nothing against Matson and the man still might be able to help him.

"You reckon the trouble between Jet and this Pardee was over the money he owed you?" Ben asked.

Matson shrugged. "It's likely. I'd like to help you more,

Mr. Webber, but no one heard just what went between Jet and Pardee. I can tell you I didn't give no orders for him to start a shootin' without cause."

Ben nodded. Matson's story, as far as it went, tied in with what the sheriff had told him. "Maybe you can tell me where the boy was buried. I'm told you made arrangements."

Matson frowned. "Well, now, I'm sorry, Mr. Webber. I did pay Luke Harris for the coffin afterwards, but I was here in my place when the boy was hanged that night. I understand he was cut down and buried as soon as he was found, but I can't just say where he was put to rest."

"I'd like to know," Ben said.

"Might I ask why?" Matson's eyes were watchful on Ben's.

"I figure to bury the boy on my own ranch nearby his mother," Ben said. "I come to take him back."

Matson stared at him, pulling thoughtfully at the long strands of his mustache. "That the only reason you come?"

"It is. It don't seem to me that's so hard to understand, Mr. Matson."

"Maybe not," Matson said. "But it's easy to understand how a man like you might also be thinkin' of gettin' back at those who didn't give your boy a chance."

"If he did what they say, I've no quarrel. He would have hanged anyway, as the sheriff says."

Matson seemed puzzled. "That may be," he admitted. "But it seems a strange kind of way for a father to feel."

Ben didn't answer. This was not something he could easily explain, nor did he feel a need to. And, thinking of the way the anger in him had turned on Luke Harris, he wondered if he'd been honest with himself all along about his motives in coming to Red Peak.

Matson put a friendly hand on Ben's shoulder. "Mr. Webber, I'd advise you against goin' through with what you're plannin'. If you try to take Jet back with you, you'll just be runnin' into trouble with the law and the town. After all, it don't really matter where a man is buried, once it's done."

Ben Webber felt dislike for Matson growing in him, a feeling stronger than should have been prompted by anything the man had said. It wasn't just that he was too free with his advice, too ready to tell a man how he should feel or what he should do. There was too much about the man that was at war with his ready smile and smooth way of talking.

"I reckon that's up to me to decide," Ben said.

Matson withdrew his hand, but he was still smiling, still friendly. "I'm not a man to tell another what he should do," he said. "But you'll be buckin' against more than one man might be able to handle right now. Sometimes things has to bide their time. And I promise you this, Mr. Webber. You needn't worry about those responsible for Jet's hangin' not payin' for it. They will, and you can rest your mind on that."

"I been tryin' to tell you, Mr. Matson," Ben said quietly, "I didn't come here to revenge my boy. But if I had that in mind, I wouldn't be leavin' it to nobody else."

For just an instant there was something deep and cold in Matson's mahogany eyes. Then it was gone and you saw only the smile.

"That's well said, sir," he declared. Abruptly his thoughts

seemed to make a switch. "But I keep forgettin'. This is your first night in our town. A man's got a right to relax and enjoy himself. Drink up, Mr. Webber!"

He gave an almost imperceptible nod to someone across the room. Ben turned to see the pretty girl he'd noticed before walking toward them. Matson leaned close to Ben's ear, lowering his voice confidentially.

"I'd like for you to enjoy a sample of Gold Nugget hospitality," he murmured. Then, more loudly, "Nothing's too good for Jet Webber's kin."

Ben's eyes were taken with the girl, but out of their corners he saw another of the women leading a drunken cowboy up a flight of steps to a balcony which ran the length of the building. Off the balcony led a number of doors. Then the girl stopped close to Ben and it was hard to look at anything else. She was even more comely than he'd thought when you saw her close, with brown eyes as big and innocent as a newborn calf's and lips pouting like they'd burst if you put your mouth to them.

"This is Mr. Webber, Julie," Matson was saying. "Jet was his son."

The girl seemed to be waiting for a signal from Matson. When she got it she looked full at Ben, her red lips beginning to part in a smile. "I'm mighty pleased to meet Jet's daddy," she said.

"My pleasure, Miss Julie," Ben said with dignity. He thought of the rooms upstairs and turned to glance at the untouched drink still sitting on the bar. Deliberately he met Matson's gaze. "Thank you for the drink," he said. "But I'll be gettin' along now."

He saw the tight set of anger around Matson's mouth as

he turned away. Indifferent to it, Ben bowed briefly to the girl and started toward the doors. If he'd thought to see annoyance in her eyes at his rebuff he was disappointed. There was reaction there but it seemed to be curiosity, and he sensed her gaze following him across the room. He had a fleeting wonder at her interest.

She was a girl for a man like Matson, he thought as he went out, and he wondered that the knowledge should nettle him.

The night was cool and the air felt clean after the stale smoke and the noise and the strong whisky smells of the saloon. Ben started walking, his mind circling slowly around the facts he'd learned. What puzzled him most was the way everyone he'd met denied knowing where Jet was buried—and everyone was anxious to have him leave Red Peak without the boy. Ben couldn't make sense of it. His thoughts kept prodding at the problem, trying to turn it over and find some answer underneath.

He was still revolving the day's events in his mind when he became vaguely aware of the fact that the ground had been rising under his feet. He paused. He'd given no direction to his feet, but now he found himself standing at the north end of town with the livery stable off to his left and the church visible on his right. Between them the powdery dust of a trail showed in the moonlight, leading around the hill. Ben knew that some part of his mind had been sending him this way.

He followed the rising curve of the hill. On its far side he found himself cut off from a view of the town and beyond reach of its sounds. He stood on the north slope of the hill, listening to the night's big silence, conscious of the immense reaches of the sky above him, a blue curtain pricked with stars, and he looked down with a stirring of emotion at the stillness of the graveyard.

Close to him on the slope, shaded by the stretching arms of a big cottonwood, were the mounds of unmarked graves. Below them where the ground leveled out small stones and crosses in orderly rows marked the resting places of other dead. In the darkness all looked the same. Maybe his mission was pointless. Maybe it didn't really matter where a man was buried. But death was a big thing, a thing beyond the scope of the mind to grasp, as great as the endless prairie of the sky. A man could deal with it only as he saw fit.

The hotel lobby was empty. A lamp flickered on the counter but no one was behind it. Ben felt the silence of the hotel and he thought it strange that a building could house so many people and yet be so still and empty-feeling. He thought without pleasure of the room waiting for him at the top of the stairs. Hotel rooms had a special loneliness. The ranch was lonely now, too, empty without Ellen, but not in this cold way. There was warmth there in the timber house, familiar things to see and touch and smell, guns to clean and dishes to wash and memories to dust off and contemplate.

The hotel room was dark. Ben closed the door and fumbled in his pocket for a match. He stopped, muscles cording with tension, feeling rather than hearing the presence of someone there in the darkness with him. A match scraped and exploded into flame.

Crouched to spring or defend himself, Ben gasped with amazement. The light of the match painted bare shoulders with a pink glow. The girl called Julie moved to touch the sputtering match flame to a lamp on the table against one wall. Its glow revealed a holster and gun belt on the table that didn't belong to Ben.

The moment's tension reacted in Ben. He spoke angrily. "I gave Matson to understand—"

"He didn't send me," the girl said quickly. "I come on my own."

Once again Ben stared in surprise. The silence lengthened, and he found himself thinking that the room was cool and the girl would be chilled with so little covering. It was not possible to be unaware of how soft her shoulders would be to the touch, how smooth the youthful skin. The knowledge that she might have been picked to entertain him in one of the little rooms off the Gold Nugget's balcony rested uncomfortably in his mind.

"I'm Julie Larkin," the girl said suddenly. "I'm sorry to surprise you so, bein' here. I should have reckoned—"

"That's all right," Ben said. He had to grin. "Though I could think of safer things you might do."

The girl's concern dissolved in a smile that lit her face like sunlight breaking through a cloud. She looked younger then and even prettier. The smile she'd worn in the Gold Nugget hadn't been real.

"I didn't put on a light," she said, growing serious and glancing toward the window, "because I thought it might be better if folks didn't know I was talkin' to you."

Ben crossed to the window and drew the yellowed shade over it. As he turned back he saw Julie shiver. Ben shrugged out of his buckskin jacket and held it out to her. She moved into it, making him hold it to fit across her shoulders. His fingers brushed against her skin, and he was aware of the pleasant scent of her.

"Thank you, Mr. Webber," she said. Her voice was low and husky with an accent Ben had heard before in folks from Georgia or thereabouts. "I suppose you're wonderin' why I'm here."

"It crossed my mind."

She faced him. Her eyes were frank and open as if to let him see the truth. "That's Jet's gun on the table. It was brought back to the Gold Nugget and Matson give it to me. I figured you might want to have it and it would rightly belong to you."

Ben looked at the gun in its holster but he made no move to examine it. It spoke with its own voice and told of things he didn't want to hear.

"I suppose you wonder why it was given to me."

Puzzled, Ben brought his eyes back to the girl. "Why?"

"I was Jet's girl," she said quietly. "We was goin' to be married."

If she'd said she had put the noose around his neck, her words could not have stunned Ben more. He was conscious of gaping at her open-mouthed.

She flushed. "I reckon you're thinkin' a man wouldn't marry a woman like me," she said, a touch of defiance in her voice. "But Jet didn't mind. He knew all there was to know about me and he didn't care. He wanted to marry me an' he kept askin' me and then I said I would."

Ben shook his head. "I wasn't thinkin' that," he said. He could see how a man could want her, could feel so strong about her he'd be willing to forget what was past and done if she'd have him. It was the news that Jet could be this man that left him wondering. Somehow he always thought of Jet as a kid with a wild, untamed streak, as a boy who got into trouble—not as a man with a man's desires and needs. Five years would have made a deal of difference. It was not a boy who had died at all, but a man Ben had never had a chance to know. He felt a sudden, keener sense of loss, as if a wound healed over had had the scab torn off and lay open, exposed to the shock of air.

"Did you know the man he killed?" Ben asked gruffly. "Did you know of anything between them?"

She hesitated. "No." Her chin tilted up and she met Ben's gaze defiantly. "But I don't believe he done it the way they say. He wouldn't kill a man that way."

The momentary excitement Ben felt dropped off sharply into disappointment. He'd hoped that she might have known of some motive that would make Pardee's murder less cold-blooded. He liked the girl's show of spirit and her loyalty to Jet, but he knew you couldn't trust a woman's judgment about a man she loved. Her faith proved only that she couldn't bring herself to believe ill of Jet.

"You don't believe what they say, do you?" she asked sharply, her tone incredulous. "You can't think that of him—your son!"

"He was seen."

"Seen! By the likes of—" She caught herself.

Alert, Ben seized her by the arms. "You know who the man was that saw the shootin'?"

"Didn't they tell you?"

He shook his head. "The sheriff figured I was huntin'

trouble. Who was it, Miss Julie? Tell me the man's name."

She looked down at his hands, and Ben became aware of gripping her hard. She was so close to him that he could feel the warmth of her body in more than his hands. He let them drop quickly.

"I'll tell you," she said. "It was Indian Joe."

Ben frowned. "An Indian?"

"No, they just call him that because he used to be a scout." Julie shrugged. "He's an old man hangs around town gettin' drinks whenever he can. He doesn't do much except help out at the stable and dig graves. They say he was in the loft of the stable when the shootin' took place out behind."

"He's the gravedigger?" Excitement stirred in Ben. "Then he'll know where Jet is buried. He's the one I've got to talk to. Where can I find him?"

"Well, he hangs around the stable mostly—he sleeps there, and that's how come he seen Jet and Pardee talkin' together and watched them." When Ben picked up his hat she reached out to catch his sleeve. "But there's no use tryin' to find him now."

Ben confronted her. "Why not?"

"He'll be sleepin' it off by now, this time of night. Joe just kind of lives for drinkin'. He was in the saloon earlier and he was far gone then. You'd best talk to him in the mornin'."

Ben hesitated, frustration warring with the knowledge that her words made sense. If the man was a drunkard there'd be no point in talking to him when he couldn't think or speak clearly. And he probably couldn't lead Ben to Jet's grave in the darkness. That would have to wait until morning.

Julie stepped in close to Ben, her big eyes searching his face. "Mr. Webber! You didn't mean what you've been sayin' about just comin' here to take Jet's body back, did you? You come to find those that hanged him, isn't that why?"

"No." The word was blunt. "If he did what they say, I've no quarrel with those who'd have him pay for it. They acted wrong, not trying him, but a man who'll break the law in killing can't expect to hide behind the law."

There was disbelief in her expression. "But you're his daddy!"

Resentment flared in him. "He didn't figure it that way! He gave no thought to his mom when she was dyin'. He left home because he killed another man and I whipped him for it!"

Julie stepped back as if he'd hit her. The flickering lamplight showed her face pale, the spots of rouge in her cheeks bright red against the white of her skin. Her full lower lip began to quiver. Tears filled the cups of her eyes to over-flowing.

Compassion made Ben step toward her, his hand reaching out to take her arm. And suddenly the tears burst forth and she was in his arms, her sobbing muffled against his chest, her body shuddering as she cried.

"Oh, Ben! I—I tried not to believe it! I tried to tell myself he couldn't have done it. I didn't want to believe!"

He held her, his hands gentle and comforting on her back, letting the tears spill out until she would empty herself of them. He understood the way she had tried to convince herself of Jet's innocence, refusing to accept what the facts told her, yet knowing deep inside that some day she'd have to face the truth. He'd done the same. Sympathy rose strong in him.

But there was something else as well, and it became more powerful as her sobbing slowly stopped and she was quiet in his arms. He made no move to release her. It had been a long time since he'd held a woman in his arms, a woman young and pretty and vibrant with life. It had been a long time since he'd felt the softness of a plump bosom warm against his chest or traced with his fingers the yielding suppleness of a woman's arching back.

She raised her face. The tears had left their trace upon her cheeks, and her eyes were moist and shining, the long, dark lashes damp. Her beauty struck him with a force to make his senses reel. Quickened sympathy gave way to a flame of feeling so long turned low and feeble that he had thought it forever extinguished.

"Oh, Ben!" she whispered.

An angry guilt engulfed him with the sudden violence of a spring flood. He thrust her away. For a moment he glared at her, his face dark as thunderclouds. He saw the doubt and uncertainty fade from her eyes. Her lips parted in a gentle, wistful smile.

"I understand," she said softly. "I wish—"

She left the words unsaid. With an impulsive quickness that caught him by surprise she darted in to him, bringing up her mouth to kiss the corner of his. Her lips were incredibly soft. He felt their imprint after she had drawn away, even after she had slipped out of his buckskin jacket and, to break a final lingering meeting of their eyes, had retreated to the door. There she turned. He saw a yearning in her face.

"Go home, Ben Webber," she said. "I wouldn't want to see you hurt. Go home."

Then she was gone. The silence pounded in his chest. He stared at the strange gun belt on the table, at the holster leather polished hard and shiny from the rubbing of metal against it. Guilt still rode him. She had been Jet's girl.

Seven

Ben rose early. The night's chill gripped the room and his teeth chattered as he quickly dressed. He rustled up a pan of cold water and shaved with it, the tough whiskers pulling hard against the straight razor edge. There was no sound of other activity in the rooms adjoining his, but when he went down the stairs and passed through the lobby the woman was already behind the counter. She didn't speak.

Outside, the street was almost empty. A man rode by in a buckboard, shoulders hunched against the cold, and another was dismounting from his horse far up the street. The sun hung low over the broad table of land to the east, giving a promise of warmth to come in the day. Ben walked briskly to work the chill out of his body. He passed the restaurant, where a lone man ate, pausing to glance up curiously as Ben went by, then bending his head back toward his plate, eating with a shoveling motion. A dog with protruding ribs darted out into the street in front of Ben, eyed him fearfully, turned to run with his long tail curling between his legs as Ben came close.

There was activity in the stable. Ben didn't see the man who had taken his horse when he arrived, but as he approached, a gnarled old man with an unkempt beard was leading a horse out to water. He turned a bright, alert glance on Ben, who stopped by the trough.

"Jeff ain't up yet," the old man said.

"You Indian Joe?"

"Ain't nobody else." The man showed no surprise that Ben should know his name. "You the fella brought the mustang in?"

"Yep," Ben said.

"I brushed him down. Right nice horse, that one."

"Thanks."

Indian Joe started to lead the watered horse back into the stable and Ben followed him. He put the horse in a stall and faced Ben, his bright gaze peering closely at Ben's face. His eyes were of the palest blue, red-rimmed now and watery. He wore patched jeans and a dirty blue shirt that was too big for him and hung loosely from his spare, bone-sharp frame.

"You'll be Webber," the old man said.

Ben nodded. "I hear tell you were witness to the killin' of Ross Pardee. I need to talk to you."

"I been 'specting you." Indian Joe spat. "Heard you was pokin' around. I buried your son."

"You'll know where then."

The pale eyes snapped like flint sparking. " 'Course! You think I'm feeble-minded that I can't remember somethin' four or five days?"

Ben's lips moved slightly on the brink of humor. "They say you like a drink or two. And a drinkin' man can some-times be forgetful."

"Well, I'll tell you now. It don't seem like drink affects me that way. Fact is"—Joe bared toothless gums in a grin and peered at Ben slyly—"it kind of stimulates my memory. Warms up my innards like, and my brain just seems to start workin' better."

"You need somethin' in your belly," Ben agreed. "I'll buy breakfast."

"Breakfast!" The old man snorted and made a sour face. "There's nothing that'll spoil good whisky more'n food will. Now suppose we jest—"

"I'm eating," Ben said. "You're welcome to come along."

"Well, I ain't et," Joe grumbled. "I tell you what. I'll eat with you if'n you'll buy a glassful afterwards to kill the taste."

Ben grinned. "It's a bargain."

They started down the street, the old man still complaining. He had to trot to keep up with Ben's long strides.

"You're the long-leggedest, soberest waddie I met since Cap'n Jack Crawford," he protested. "Next thing you'll be spoutin' poetry."

Ben stopped in his tracks. "You knew Jack Crawford?"

Joe's beard quivered indignantly. "Knew him? Hell, I taught him most of what he knew about scoutin'. Let me tell you, I knew 'em all, son. I rode with 'em and fought with 'em, and many's the time I come close to dyin' with 'em. Those were the times!"

"I rode with the Fifth Cavalry for a spell after the war," Ben said. "Might be our paths crossed then."

"Well, I'm damned!" Joe said. His eyes glistened with a faraway look as if they were searching the brow of a mesa for a speck of movement or seeking out the warning plume of smoke on the distant horizon. "There were some men in those days. So you rode with the Fifth!"

They walked on more slowly. Familiar names and places were exchanged with the enthusiasm of men who remember a good time, hard and demanding, and survived to tell of it. Inwardly Ben had to grin at the legendary prowess of Indian Joe's career. To hear him tell of it, he'd been there at the bloody battle of Beecher Island and he cursed with regret that he'd just missed being massacred at Bighorn. He'd been known and respected and feared by such as Red Cloud and Crazy Horse of the Sioux and Yellow Hand of the Cheyenne, and he gave them grudging admiration in his turn as brave warriors and brilliant leaders—worthy opponents for Indian Joe and the rugged men whose names he linked with his—Old Bill Williams and Jim Bridger and Tom Fitzpatrick and Poet Jack Crawford. Ben discounted for the exaggerations most men make and saw the core of truth behind the old man's words. As they talked the two men warmed to each other, the old man seeking in Ben's recollections a confirmation of memories growing dimmer, and Ben recognizing and understanding Joe's attempt to cling to the pride and prowess of the past, setting them against the present when his useful time was over.

They were the only ones in the restaurant. Indian Joe wolfed his food, grumbling bitterly, interrupting his complaints to speak of an incident suddenly remembered, brought from a dark corner of the past and held up to the light of capricious memory, an incident of great courage or strength or endurance. Often it was a feat of vision Joe remembered.

"General Crook used to say," the old man boasted, "that I could spot war paint farther off than any man who'd ever served under him. Maybe there wasn't much to the rest of me, leastwise not in size, but I could see farther and better'n any Indian."

Looking into the shining blue eyes, Ben gave credence to the claim, sensing that Joe's eagle eye was a point of special pride with him. He let Joe eat and talk, not pushing him, knowing he'd come in time to the thing which crowded all else out of Ben's mind. The moment came when they were drinking coffee, the old man forgetting to complain about the taste. Joe turned the pale eyes on Ben's face, squinting slightly.

"I wasn't at the hangin'," Joe said. "Don't know who was, far as that goes. But I seen your boy go against Pardee, who never even got a chance to draw. His gun was still in its holster when he died."

"You're sure of that?" Ben asked woodenly.

"He killed him," Joe insisted. "There's no use tryin' to pretend he didn't. Happened out behind the stable. About dusk it was. I was up in the loft an' that's how I come to see them. An' I was sober, too," he added quickly.

Ben said nothing. The hope that had been struggling to grow in him, nurtured in spite of his doubts by Julie's words the night before, began to shrivel. He liked Indian Joe. It didn't stand to reason the old man would lie to him. He had nothing to gain by it.

"You didn't hear words between them?" he asked.

"Nope. Weren't close enough for listenin'. But I knowed it was Jet Webber—he always wore that black shirt and hat of his. Nobody looked like him. An' I seen the dead man up close just before he died."

Ben frowned slightly. He wondered at Joe's emphasis on

identifying Jet. "Pardee didn't speak?"

"Nope. Gut-shot, he was. He wasn't fit for talkin' when I got to him. Young Webber was gone off by then." Joe paused. "Only thing I couldn't figure was how the posse caught him so quick and easy. I wouldn't have figured him to walk into a rope without takin' a couple of men with him, not the way he was with a gun."

For a moment Ben was silent. This was what he had had to know, that the story of Jet's deed and his punishment was true. He felt no murderous rage against the men of the posse. They'd taken a life in exchange for a life. It was a code Ben knew and acknowledged.

"You dug his grave," Ben said heavily.

"Yep. That same night he was cut down an' they come an' woke me up." He looked at Ben apologetically. "Most men don't take to diggin'. I'll do it for a bottle."

"I'd like you to show me where."

They left the restaurant. Passing the saloon, Joe grabbed Ben's arm. "How about that drink? You bargained for it."

Ben nodded. It didn't matter to him now, a few minutes more or less. He didn't even object when Joe poured himself a second glass, the bartender having unwarily left the bottle within reach. The Gold Nugget was almost empty at this hour of the morning, and John Matson wasn't in sight. As Ben and Joe pushed away from the bar and started toward the swinging doors two men stepped inside, barring the way. Ben recognized the thickset, redheaded gunman he'd seen in the bar the night before. His companion was Mexican, a slim, graceful man with gleaming white teeth and a knife scar along one cheek. Insolently they took their time, forcing Ben and Joe to wait for them to get out of the way.

"Mornin', boys," Indian Joe said cheerfully as he stepped around them.

Ben hesitated, meeting the redhead's cold-eyed stare, before he followed Joe through the doors. When they were in the street the old man glanced up thoughtfully at the hard line of Ben's mouth.

"Them's two of Matson's boys," he said. "Red Morrell is big, but I'd bet he's soft in the belly. Not like we was in the old days. That Chico, though, he's different. They say he'll fight like an Indian with a knife."

Ben thought of Matson's glib explanation for surrounding himself with hired killers. The man wasn't to be trusted in anything he said, but the fact seemed unimportant after Indian Joe's testimony against Jet.

The old man stepped out more jauntily after the two drinks. Ben reckoned there was so much liquor in Joe it took only a drink or two to activate the residue left over. They walked together in silence now, Ben only half-listening to the old man's off-key humming of a campfire ballad that had to do with how much better off a man was without a woman to saddle him with words and worries. The town was waking, stores opening their doors and a scattering of riders kicking up dust in the street. Somewhere a blacksmith's hammer rang off metal, and the shrill clamor of children at play pierced the morning air. The sun was fulfilling its earlier promise and the morning coolness no longer had any bite.

Joe trotted along briskly, as if to prove he could match Ben's pace. They left the town and the stable and the church behind them, blocked off soon by the bulk of the hill at the north end of town. There was a moment when Red Peak was in sight, alive with activity under the bright sun, and then a moment later the two men plunged into cool shadow and a strange stillness where even the birds were silent and the leaves of the big cottonwood hung limp, unmoved by any breeze. The graveyard was spread out below them.

"Which one is it?" Ben asked quietly.

Indian Joe darted a quick glance at him and licked his lips. He peered then at the nearer graves set into the slope. He started down among them, Ben at his heels. Close to the base of the hill was the freshly turned earth of a recent grave. Ben's heartbeat quickened. Then Joe veered away from it. He stopped suddenly and looked around, frowning. His face brightened.

"That'll be it!" Joe declared.

He pointed toward a mound some twenty feet away. Ben's gaze followed the direction indicated by the gnarled finger. The grave was one in a row just above them where the slope began to rise.

"You're sure?" Ben asked.

"Yep. The preacher, Mr. Templeton, he wouldn't have taken kindly to my diggin' down on the flat. Figures some of his folk wouldn't rest easy with a killer amongst 'em. No offense, Mr. Webber."

"No," Ben said in a flat voice. "I wouldn't want you to point out the wrong one, Joe."

"What's that mean?" the old man said indignantly. "You tryin' to say I can't pick out what I dug myself? That's the one, all right!"

He started toward it. He'd taken no more than two steps

when he stumbled over a projection of thick root from the big cottonwood. Swearing, Joe scrambled to keep his feet. Ben made no move. Suspicion turned into conviction, and his hands clenched as he tried to control the quick thrust of anger.

"I told you!" Joe cried. "This is the one!"

Ben walked forward slowly. Joe crouched beside a grave on which the overturned earth had crusted. Even at a distance it had showed to Ben the signs of having been washed and smoothed by rain. A few green shoots of grass pushed up to break through the crust of dirt.

"It's old," Ben said tightly. "Weeks old."

"What? What are you tryin' to—" Joe's querulous retort broke off. He licked his lips again. "You think so? Well, maybe you're right. I could be wrong. It was night and dark."

"They were mighty anxious to get him buried," Ben said thoughtfully. "Who were they, Joe?"

"It was dark," the old man repeated uneasily. "I couldn't say for sure."

Ben studied him without replying. He'd expected the evasion.

"There's so many of them," Joe said, squinting at the rows of graves. "Buried a stranger here last week. Then there was John—he was the barber—got into a fight." He took a few quick steps toward another mound, bending to peer closely at it. "This could be it. No—that one, maybe."

He started to run forward. Puzzled and angry, Ben watched him. For the first time he noticed that Joe had a way of holding one hand out before him, but the old man failed to see the mound of another grave not set even with the others. Joe tripped and fell heavily. He lay where he had fallen.

Ben ran over to him, understanding jelling suddenly. He reached down and none too gently hauled Joe to his feet. Angrily the old man tried to twist free of Ben's grip.

"What's that for? What are you doin'? I don't need no help. You think I'm too old to get up myself?"

"You don't see very good," Ben said flatly.

"That's a lie!" The denial was hot with anger. "I can see better'n any man—better'n you! I couldn't get around the way I do less'n I could see!"

"You know the town," Ben snapped. "That's why you fooled me. I suppose you know every stick of it. But out here it's different, isn't it? The graves all look the same. And the land keeps changing shape so you keep fallin' over things."

"Any man can trip," Joe retorted, thrusting Ben's hands away. "All right, maybe I can't find your boy's buryin' place. A man can't always remember. But don't you go sayin' I can't see, you hear?"

The pale blue eyes glared fiercely at Ben. Disappointment was heavy in Ben as he returned the old man's stare. He'd counted on Joe's knowledge.

"How could you see Jet draw on the other man, Joe?" Ben asked softly. "How could you be sure? It was dusk, you said. A man would need keen eyes to be sure. Eyes like yours used to be."

"I saw him!" Joe said angrily. "Don't try to trip me up with words. Maybe my eyes ain't so good as they once was, but they're still good enough to recognize a man as close as Jet Webber was to me. Besides, I'd seen the two of them earlier together. Arguin', they was. That wasn't long before the shootin', either."

"Are you sure you didn't just hear some shots and run out to find Pardee dyin'?"

"Nope," Joe said stubbornly. "I seen your boy draw, an' I heard the shots. He called out, Webber did, and when Pardee turned he drew on him. I seen Pardee drop. I got out there soon as I could. By then Pardee was almost gone and your boy wasn't anywheres to be seen."

There was a ring of truth in the old man's insistence. And maybe he could see enough to be accurate in his report of the shooting. Still he made a poor witness to justify a hanging.

As to the grave, either Joe had been too drunk or too blind at night to tell where he dug. Ben would have to find another way of locating it.

The old man was glaring at him defensively. Ben kept his face expressionless, careful now to keep the pity out of his gaze. A man needed at least one thing to take pride in. You couldn't blame Joe for trying to hang onto that one thing even after it was gone. What was a scout without his eyes?

Ben turned his back on the old man and started to walk away, the gesture suggesting more anger than he was able to sustain against Joe. He'd taken a half dozen steps when the old man's voice called out.

"Mr. Webber! Wait now!"

Ben turned. Joe was trotting toward him. "It's the truth what I said about the shootin'," the old man said earnestly. "An' I did bury your boy. Maybe I didn't tell you all that—"

A shot cracked out, and the leaves chattered in the cottonwood directly overhead. As he dropped flat Ben saw Joe diving to the ground behind the tree. Ben rolled, not wanting to offer a still target, berating himself for coming out without the Winchester. He slid behind a mound of earth that offered partial protection and lay quiet.

The shot had come from the cover of trees and bushes to the west of the graveyard. A rifle by the sound of it, Ben thought. He scanned the area, but no telltale puff of smoke or glint of metal was visible. Seconds ticked by. There was no second shot. Ben crawled to his right, his eyes on the brush from which the shot had come. There the ground was slightly higher, and a man with a rifle could pin them down as long as he liked. Ben was surprised when his movements drew no fire. A crease of perplexity deepened in his forehead. A lot of men shot wild, but that first bullet hadn't been fired from so far off that it should have missed them by so much. And the failure to follow it up made it seem more like a warning than—

He glanced sharply at Indian Joe. The old man's pale blue eyes were wide, staring at Ben's face. He hadn't moved from the protection of the tree. One hand kept jumping in an involuntary spasm. Ben wondered suddenly what kind of fear a man would feel when he could no longer defend himself against a gun, when his eyes were so dim he couldn't see his enemy even in the open. . . .

"What were you gonna tell me?" Ben called in a low voice.

Joe licked his lips. "Nothin'," he said quickly. "Jest that I been tellin' you the truth. That's all I was tryin' to say. I can't tell you nothin' more."

Slowly Ben pushed himself to his feet. He had a feeling

there was no longer any danger. He stared down at the old man for a long moment.

"I reckon we might as well go back," he said.

Eight

They walked back to the stable in silence. Ben shrugged off the temptation to try to scout out the man who'd shot at them. Unarmed, he could accomplish little, and in any event he was sure the man had slipped away. Indian Joe kept glancing nervously over his shoulder at first, but when nothing happened his confidence returned. By the time they'd reached the stable his shaggy beard was bristling with a wordless belligerence.

Joe brought out the mustang at Ben's request and hunted up a saddle Ben could borrow, moving with a careless quickness that was meant to give the lie to Ben's suspicions about his eyesight. Joe's actions had their effect. It was hard to believe that a man could get around so well if he were as half-blind as Ben had concluded the old man was. Joe must be able to see enough to make things out even though he hadn't been able to find the grave he'd dug for Jet. Ben couldn't convince himself that Joe would label Jet Webber a killer unless he was sure of it, but he was positive that the old man knew more than he had told and that he was about to say more when the shot frightened him into silence.

Mounting the mustang, Ben looked down at Joe. "How do I find the Pardee ranch?" he asked.

Surprise robbed Joe of his angry defiance. "You're figurin' to ride out there?"

"I owe it to the man's sister," Ben said. "Besides, she might know of somethin' between Jet and her brother."

The old man appeared dubious, but he seemed anxious to seize the chance of talking on safe ground. "She won't welcome you. That is, if Matson hasn't run her off the place already. An' he won't find that's so easy with Miss Nancy. Not if she's a mind to stay."

The words conjured up a picture of a tough-minded, stubborn frontier woman. Ben had known the type and he had a respect for them. "Where is the place?" he repeated.

Joe shrugged. "You'll find it if you ride due west. There's a valley beyond that first big range of hills. Pardee had his place up at the narrow end of the valley to the north. Matson owns most of the rest of it," the old man added pointedly.

Ben nodded. As he swung away and rode into town, Indian Joe peered after him, and Ben wondered when the point was reached where he and the horse became a meaningless blur in the old man's failing sight. It might be important to know. . . .

He tethered the horse outside the hotel while he went up for his Winchester and a canteen of water. His eye was caught by the gun belt still lying on the table. It was a kind of symbol of the bitter truth you couldn't get away from no matter what else happened. Ben wondered idly if the gun was the only reason Julie Larkin had come to his room. It took an effort to pull his thoughts away from her.

He went down to the street. While he was fitting the rifle scabbard to the horse he glanced up to see Jake Howell bearing down on him purposefully. Ben finished attaching the leather sheath and slipped the rifle into it, checking to make sure it was firm and steady.

"You figure to take my advice now, Mr. Webber?" the sheriff spoke behind him.

"What advice was that?"

Howell's heartiness was gone and the surly tone of his voice now matched the look in his dark-bearded face. "I give you warning," he said. "I played fair with you right from the start. And you just went right ahead and started makin' trouble for yourself. Luke Harris told me—"

"He threatened me with an ax," Ben interrupted. "I took it away from him."

"You like to broke his arm!"

"That's his lookout," Ben said quietly.

"Now look here!" Howell said angrily. "You can't jest come ridin' into town and start pushin' people around because they don't take kindly to you. We got ways of dealin' with folks like that."

"The way you dealt with Jet Webber?" Ben asked, his voice cold and hard, his gaze level and unfriendly on the sheriff's face.

Howell looked away. "I told you I didn't have nothin' to do with the hangin'," he said aggrievedly, his manner changing. "There's no call to get excited. I jest don't want no more trouble here, Mr. Webber. And the way you been pokin' around, you're bound to meet it."

"You know why I'm here," Ben said quietly.

"And I told you it was agin the law!" The sheriff's narrow eyes grew suddenly suspicious. "Did Joe show you where the boy was buried?"

"He couldn't find it. Though he might have if somebody hadn't taken a shot at us."

"A shot!" Clearly startled, the sheriff stared at Ben. "Now dammit, that's jest what I been sayin'. Now maybe you'll listen to me."

Ben interrupted him. "Joe doesn't see very good, does he, Sheriff?"

Howell's gaze shifted to the street, avoiding Ben's. "He sees clear enough for most things. And Joe's word is good enough for me. If he says he saw the shootin', there ain't a man in town will doubt him." The sheriff's eyes moved up again to find Ben's. "Now that you know what I told you was the facts, you'll be wise to ride right out of town before there's any more shootin'."

"Not yet awhile," Ben said curtly. He swung up into the saddle. "Maybe Miss Pardee can tell me why Jet might have shot her brother."

Ben thought he saw quick alarm in the sheriff's eyes. "You're not ridin' out to talk to her!"

"Yep."

"Why? There's nothin' she can tell you about what happened."

"Maybe not. But I owe her my respects, Sheriff."

"Now you listen to me, Mr. Webber. You'd best leave well enough alone. Miss Nancy's grievin'. She won't take kindly to another Webber ridin' in there, and that's a fact. Besides, she's fixin' to leave the place. It belongs to John Matson now." He paused. "Her hands have already left."

Ben frowned. "Is she there alone?"

Howell looked uncomfortable. "Her foreman's still there. The others quit, the way I hear. Mr. Matson rode out to tell her she could stay on a spell—now you have to admit that's decent—but she run him off. Wouldn't even talk to him."

"Well, maybe she'll talk to me," Ben said, turning the horse. "There's things about this shootin' don't make sense. I aim to find out why."

Howell grabbed angrily at the mustang's reins, causing the horse to shy nervously. "Dammit, man, I won't have it! She's like as not to put a bullet through you!"

Ben controlled the horse. His smile was cold. "That would make it easier for everybody, wouldn't it? Then you wouldn't have to tell me why you're so all-fired anxious I don't find Jet's body."

The sheriff's eyes got even smaller and meaner, and his skin flushed dark under the black beard. "You won't listen, Mr. Webber. I tried to give you good advice but you won't listen. Now I tell you this. You better heed what I say. If Indian Joe can't tell you where your boy is buried, there ain't nobody can. An' if you try to go diggin' up the grave-yard huntin' you'll be put under arrest. Now that's fair warning, Mr. Webber!"

Ben eyed him calmly. He was thinking that the sheriff seemed to be too fond of giving fair warning. His threats lacked conviction.

"I heard you, Sheriff," Ben said. "That's all I seem to have heard since I came to Red Peak—warnings. You folks are mighty anxious to help a stranger stay out of trouble. I'm powerful grateful." He took a deep breath. It was a long speech for him. "Maybe I'm just stubborn, Sheriff, not to heed all this good advice. But it's going to take more than words to stop me doin' what I came for!"

He dug his heels into the mustang's belly. The horse leaped forward, breaking the sheriff's hold on the reins. Then it was running free, the explosion of its hooves blotting out the sheriff's angry shout at Ben's fast retreating back.

Once out of town he rode on without hurrying, letting the mustang find its own pace through the rough climbing, urging it into an easy trot where the land leveled out. Two hours' ride brought him to the crest of a range of hills. The trail topped the last rise suddenly and he looked down at a green valley lying between this and the next rocky barrier of higher mountains. The valley was long and narrow, running north and south between the protecting banks of the hills. It was shaped something like a Mexican jug, wider and fatter at the near end, narrowing toward the distant pass to the north. A stream cut across the fat belly of the valley, a river swollen now by the spring drainage from the hills but one that would probably dry to a thin trickle in two months' time. The wider plateau with the stream in it was the better land, Ben thought, surveying the valley. Matson owned most of that. But the Pardee ranch, which must cross the valley floor at the north end, was as strategically located as the stopper on a bottle. If that north pass made an easy exit from the valley, it was easy to see why Matson would want it. He wasn't the kind of man who would like to be beholden to his neighbors for the right to cross their land.

Ben angled down toward the valley bottom, reaching it at a point above the river so he wouldn't have to ford the high-running water. It took him the better part of an hour to make the upper end of the valley. Here the land was more broken and rocky, and good grazing grass was sparse. Even if he'd had the water, Pardee couldn't have run more than a small herd.

The ranch wasn't hard to find. There was a small barn, a narrow bunkhouse, and the house itself, the buildings clustered close together in a clearing protected by a sheer face of rock that rose behind. The clearing was on slightly higher ground than the valley floor to the south, so that it commanded a view of the approaches to it. The site had been well chosen. Ben rode in openly. The ranch lay quiet in the sun with no sign of anyone moving about, but he had the feeling he was being watched.

He saw the spurt of smoke from a window before the crack of a rifle shot reached him. The bullet kicked up flakes of rock a safe distance to Ben's left and whined off harmlessly. Ignoring it, he kept the mustang's pace steady at an easy walk, heading directly for the ranch house from which the shot had come. There was no further warning.

He reined in close to the covered porch which spanned the length of the house. For a moment he tried without success to peer through the curtained windows. As he started to swing down from the saddle, the long barrel of a rifle pushed through the door and covered him.

"I wouldn't do that!" a woman's voice called sharply. "You can just keep right on riding."

Ben eased erect again in the saddle. He waited for the woman to come out. There was a faint prickling of the hairs at the back of his neck, for you could never tell what a grieving woman might do, but he made no move to obey her command.

She stepped out suddenly onto the porch. "You heard me!" she snapped. "Keep going!"

Ben stared at her in surprise. He'd expected a much older woman, and Indian Joe's comment had prepared him for someone rough and hard and plain. There was strength in Nancy Pardee all right, but it was sheathed in the softness of a beautiful woman not yet thirty years of age. Her face had a clean, scrubbed look that Ben liked. She wore a checked shirt tucked into tight jeans, emphasizing the narrowness of waist and hips, the full woman's swelling above. Her hair was a rich brown and curly.

At the moment her mouth was a tight line and her eyes flashed with anger. "You deaf?" she demanded. "I told you to ride on!"

"I heard you," Ben said. "You're Miss Pardee?"

"As if you didn't know who I was!"

"It stood to reason," he said calmly.

She checked a retort. For a moment she seemed disconcerted. The barrel of the rifle began to lower. Then her mouth tightened again, and the gun swung up. "You'll be one of Matson's men," she said. "Though you don't talk like one. You can go back and tell him I won't be run off this place. I'll leave all right enough, but I'll go when I'm ready to."

Ben saw the pride in the lift of her chin, the defiance expressed in every line of her body—the firm way she planted her feet, the businesslike steadiness of the rifle pointing at his chest, the unwavering watchfulness of her eyes. And he thought he could see the hurt, too. A darkness showed under her eyes, the way a woman will appear when she's shed tears, and her face had a fine-drawn look, not sullen or self-pitying but marked by grief that wasn't meant for display.

"I've not come from Matson," Ben said quietly.

The rifle didn't waver. "You're a stranger to me," Nancy

Pardee said. "And the only strangers that come to Red Peak these days and start nosing around are Matson's hired killers."

"That may be, but I'm not one of them."

Something in the quiet honesty of Ben's voice and manner penetrated her suspicion. Her eyes flicked over him, noting the absence of a pistol at his hip, the weathered hat and dress of the cowman.

"Then who are you?" she asked, her tone less hostile but still not welcoming. "State your business. You didn't ride out here to pay a friendly call, and everyone hereabouts knows I'm not hiring."

Ben hesitated. It wasn't easy to put into words his reason for coming. "I'm Ben Webber," he said bluntly.

At first the name meant nothing to her and her face showed puzzlement. Then incredulity leaped full-blown into her eyes.

"It was my son shot your brother," Ben said.

Her face flinched as if he'd struck her. For a moment it seemed frozen, the way a blow will leave the flesh numb before the pain jumps in. Then the sudden paleness of her cheeks turned to pink and her eyes struck sparks.

"Why did you come here?"

Ben groped for the words. "I come to give my sympathies," he said. "I guess nothin' I can say will help much, but—"

"Get out!" The harsh command slashed through Ben's fumbling words. "Get out before I shoot!"

"You've no call for that," Ben said.

"What did you expect? Did you think I'd welcome you? Did you expect I'd say, 'Thank you, Mr. Webber, it's mighty nice to meet you'?" Her voice shook. "Your son killed Ross! He was my only kin—"

Tears broke out suddenly on her face. She fought them back. Ben felt her sorrow and pain as if it were his own, cutting keen and hot and deep into him. But he couldn't find the words that might express what he felt so that she could understand.

"I wanted to learn why it happened," Ben said woodenly.

"Ask John Matson! He can tell you!"

"He claims not."

"He claims not!" She flung his words back at him heavy with scorn. "Do you think he'd say he had a part in it?"

"I'm sorry, Miss Pardee. I've no wish to bring things back to you that had best be forgotten, but if Jet killed Pardee the way they say, I had to find out why."

"Why? What is there to know about why? He was hired for it, Mr. Webber. That was his job!"

"You can't be sure that's how it happened—unless you know more than I've found out."

"I don't have to know any more. He was a killer! Ross stood in Matson's way, so he had to die." She bit her lip and the marks showed white. "That was what your Jet was good for. He was good at killing. How many others have there been?"

"I don't know—"

"You ought to know! A father ought to know how many men his son kills. Do you always ride up after and say how sorry you are?"

Her cry, sharp-edged with anguish, bit into him like barbed wire snagging and tearing flesh, leaving raw wounds behind that smarted and stung. And every movement his mind made to evade the cutting truth of her words only caused them to bite deeper. It didn't help to think that it was unjust for her to turn her anger against him. Was it unjust at all?

He tried to cling to a thread of hope. "Your brother clashed with Matson. He was lookin' for trouble—"

"Ross was a fighter, Mr. Webber—but not with a gun. Your boy knew that!"

"But something must have happened between them, some reason for the shooting."

"You named the reason. There's no need to hunt around for another. Ross was one of the only men in this territory with the courage to face up to Matson. That's why he had to be killed. What other reason do you need? Your Jet was a gun, that's all. When he was pointed at somebody and told to shoot, he shot. A gun doesn't need a reason to go off, Mr. Webber. All you do is pull the trigger!"

She stopped, glaring at him, breathing hard. Ben's face was stony. Her hot words had burned away the hope he'd built up unconsciously in his mind, the pretense that he might discover some motive that would justify Jet for what he had done. Now he knew that he had only been fooling himself. That was why he'd been so eager to latch onto the mystery of the whereabouts of Jet's grave. He'd hoped without warrant that the mystery went deeper, that behind it was an answer that would change or soften the truth. But truth was a thing you couldn't change no matter how much you tried to pretend. Jet Webber had been a murderer. He'd deserved to die on the end of a rope. And Ben must share his guilt.

"I'm sorry, Miss Pardee," Ben said. The words came out

flat and meaningless, without the power to comfort.

The woman's face looked empty now, as if the flood of words had drained all the anger out of her. "Get," she said tonelessly. "Get or I'll pull this trigger."

"He was my son," Ben said, as if the fact might explain everything.

"I'll count to three." She raised the rifle to her shoulder. "One—"

"You needn't bother countin'."

He swung away. With unwonted force he kicked the mustang into motion. He didn't look back, yet he carried away in his mind a picture of the woman standing there on the long porch, a woman slim and straight and lovely, her eyes dark with sorrow and the sense of loss.

Nine

Ben rode all afternoon. Part of it was aimless riding, trying to work out the soreness in his mind, but the wounds were too raw and deep. Time, instead of healing, merely aggravated them. He left the valley by the north-end pass and circled back in the general direction of Red Peak. It was dark by the time he reached town. His body felt punished by the long solitary ride, but he was conscious only of the mind's ache of memory that wouldn't be smothered or soothed or blotted out by lesser pain.

He left the horse at the stable. Indian Joe wasn't around. Ben walked slowly toward the hotel. Passing the Gold Nugget, he noticed Luke Harris glaring at him balefully from the boardwalk, his arm in a sling. The carpenter's hostility didn't seem important any more. Ben wondered why he'd felt it necessary to beat the man down and take his ax away. He'd been proving something a man didn't need to prove. Bitter sorrow had been eating at him since the time he'd left Fort Worth. He'd had to strike out at somebody and Harris gave him an excuse.

The hotel room still held the day's heat and dust. Ben lit the lamp on the table and was suddenly motionless, staring at the gun which lay there, the long match burning out between his fingers. *Your Jet was a gun, that's all. . . . A gun doesn't need a reason to go off, Mr. Webber. All you do is pull the trigger!*

Ben fingered the smooth leather of the gun belt Jet had worn. He slid the long-barreled Colt from the holster and balanced it in his hand. Why should he have expected notches? Men talked of putting down a mark for each victim, but few men did it. Only the swaggering killers, the braggarts. There was no way of telling how many times this hammer had dropped to send hot lead tearing into yielding flesh.

A father ought to know how many men his son kills. The barbed words had stuck in his mind. He couldn't tear them loose.

Violently he jammed the gun into its holster and flung it back on the table. He was struck with the absurdity of his mission. An old man with a bleeding heart. For what? Matson had been right. It didn't matter where a man was buried. The preacher, too, had been right. A killer renounces God's mercy. Or a father's.

He went out. There was a confusion of noises and music and laughter coming from the Gold Nugget. Ben moved toward the sounds. The emptiness in him cried out to be filled. He pushed his way inside and found a place at the crowded bar. A knot of men were gathered around a tall and handsome piano against the wall. Ben hadn't noticed it before. The men were poking and prodding at it as if they were buying horseflesh. A thin little fellow in a striped shirt and a funny little round hat was trying to keep the hands away.

"Keep your hands off there, I tell you," he pleaded.

Ben turned away. His eyes were drawn to the naked woman in the big painting behind the bar. Another drinker nearby raised his glass toward the voluminous pink figure.

"Here's to Rosie," he said. "Bless her!"

Ben drank and waited for the glass to be refilled. Rosie. The painting was unnamed, but a man would dredge up his own name from somewhere in his past. Men liked to label things and people and deeds. It wasn't the thing they labeled, but themselves.

A few tinkling sounds came from the piano. There was a shout of approval. When Ben turned, the little man with the bowler hat was sitting on a stool before the piano, making a show of flexing his fingers.

"Stand back! Give him room!"

Ben saw Julie Larkin coming down the stairs alone from the balcony. She saw him watching her and stopped suddenly. She glanced up toward the top of the stairs and quickly brought her gaze back. Ben sensed a nervousness in her. Then she was smiling and coming down the steps and starting toward him.

The pianist began to play, but the music was drowned out by the immediate applause and shouting and stamping of heavy-booted feet. John Matson appeared through an office door and shoved through the crowd toward the piano, waving his hands to quiet the hubbub.

"Evenin', Mr. Webber," Julie said. He could hardly hear her words above the shouting.

"—Miss Julie."

She smiled up at him. She wore the same frilly black dress that left her shoulders bare and dipped low to her bosom. Ben felt a tug of obscure remorse, remembering the feelings she had so strongly aroused in him when she had come to his room the night before.

"—our new piano," she was saying.

"Fine," Ben said. "Mighty fine."

"It just came today. All the way from St. Louis."

The noise began to quiet somewhat. "Let him play!" John Matson was shouting. "You hear? How can he play less'n you keep quiet?" Others joined their cries to his. "Shut up!" "Quiet, damn you!" "Let him play!" Gradually the shouting faded out. A sudden silence came then, a breathless waiting. The first note sounded. There was an audible sighing. The tinkling music filled the room, giving voice to a slow and melancholy song men sang at night or when they were lonely. All around the saloon rough cowboys stood transfixed, listening with their faces slack in rapt attention. Ben too was silent, moved by the familiar sentiments and the magic of sound coaxed from the piano by the little man's skilled fingers. When he finished, the silence held for a minute while the last note lingered. There was a burst of applause.

Ben emptied his glass and pushed it back across the bar. He looked at Julie and her eyes met his. The whisky lit a fire in his empty belly. He remembered he'd not eaten since morning.

"You're drinkin' heavy," Julie said, her gaze questioning.

Ben shrugged. "It's my last night here," he said. "I'm leaving."

He saw the surprise start in her eyes, shading quickly into disbelief. "You've found Jet's grave?" she asked, keeping her voice low.

"No. It doesn't matter."

"Ben Webber, you'll not make me believe you're leavin' without him now!"

"Why not?" The bartender sloshed more whisky into Ben's glass and he picked it up. His hand was steady. "I wasn't seein' straight before."

The pianist was playing a livelier song. One man knew some of the words and he tried to sing them in a hoarse voice, sparking guffaws. The room was noisier now, but not so turbulent you couldn't hear the music. Some men drifted back to the card tables while others grouped around the piano. Ben saw John Matson weaving through the crowd toward him and Julie.

"Well, Mr. Webber!" Matson said amiably. "I see you and Julie have got acquainted after all."

"We did," Ben agreed, wondering if Matson could know that the girl had come to his room. He was surprised to find that dislike for Matson no longer rose in him. Here was the man who'd pointed the gun at Pardee and as good as pulled the trigger. If Jet was bad, this man was worse, without the courage or the cunning to do his own killing. But Ben felt nothing. He might have been a dead man the way he felt. There was only the gnawing emptiness, and the whisky would fill that.

"I hear tell you rode out to see Miss Pardee," Matson commented, looking idly away as if the statement bore no importance.

"I had a long ride," Ben said, "for little talk."

"She's still grievin' over Ross," Matson said. "And she's apt to say things she doesn't mean. But she's a mighty fine woman, Mr. Webber, and I wouldn't want you to think different. Before this trouble rose over what Ross owed me, we were right friendly. Julie can tell you that."

"That's true," Julie said. "Ross Pardee was a gamblin' man and often here."

Ben heard the words, but they meant nothing to him. The redness of Julie Larkin's mouth meant more, the whiteness of her shoulders. But these too were not for him.

"You had no trouble?" Matson asked. "Miss Nancy's kind of handy with that rifle of hers."

"No trouble," Ben said. He drank, emptying his glass again. "Though she wasn't exactly friendly." He was thinking that Matson was curious and trying not to show it.

"Mr. Webber says he's leavin'," Julie said to Matson. "Without Jet."

"You're leavin'?" Matson's tone showed only mild surprise. "Changed your mind kind of sudden, didn't you, Mr. Webber?"

The raucous chorus of shouts and stamping feet burst out, as the piano vibrated with a final triumphant chord. A man pushed out of the crowd around the remarkable instrument and caught sight of Julie. "Miss Julie!" he yelled. "Come and sing a song for us!" Others took up the cry. Ben saw the quick exchange of glances between the girl and Matson, and his faint nod.

"Go ahead, Julie. We'd all like to hear you sing for us."
He put a soft, friendly hand on Ben's arm. "Isn't that right,
Mr. Webber?"

Ben nodded. He'd like to hear her sing. She hesitated.
Ben thought he saw anxiety in the flicker of a glance she
gave him before she turned. Cheers greeted her progress
toward the piano, and the crowd of men parted to make an
aisle for her.

"I see your glass is empty," Matson said. "What do you
say to joining me for a drink at my table?"

"Don't mind," Ben said. He wanted to see where
Matson's curiosity would lead him, but that wasn't really
important. The emptiness inside him still gnawed. The fire
he'd begun to build with the whisky was too feeble. Red
Morrell, the gunslinger whose shock of flaming hair gave
him his nickname, was sitting at the table Matson led him
to. Matson jerked his thumb, and the hefty gunman eased
out of his chair. There was insolence in his stare at Ben, as
if he were laughing at him for some secret reason.
Unmoved, Ben took the vacated chair.

The bartender hurried over to the table with a fresh
bottle. As Matson broke it open and started to fill two
glasses, Julie Larkin began to sing. The room was quiet.
Ben could hear the whisky pouring and the clink of the
bottle against the lip of the glass. Then there was nothing
but the girl's voice, clear and pure.

Julie had a husky way of talking that wasn't like a young
girl at all, having too much knowledge in it, but now, across
the room, her voice rose in song with all of the lightness
and joy of youth. She looked small and slender and innocent, the make-up on her face taking on at this distance and

in the uneven light the fresh pink bloom of excitement. Ben felt the delicious tremor of her voice cutting through to him like a knife honed razor-sharp. She sang a rollicking tune about a man on a sorrel horse and a girl in a calico dress. Ben hardly heard the words, but he couldn't tear his eyes away from Julie.

The song ended and she was blotted from his sight by the horde of men swarming around her, shouting and whistling and cheering.

"She's mighty pretty, ain't she?" Matson said, leaning toward him across the table.

Ben turned. He knew the hunger had been showing in his face. "There's no denyin' that," he said, reaching for the glass at his elbow.

He drained the glass. Matson held out the bottle and refilled it. Julie was singing another song, but the men around her joined in, their booming, rasping voices smothering hers so that only once in a while did a crystal note shine through.

"What made you change your mind about stayin'?" Matson asked. "I hope it was nothin' Nancy Pardee said."

Ben shrugged. "I came to see it didn't matter," he said. "Just like you said."

But it *had* been Nancy Pardee who had made him begin to think straight, sharpening for him the picture of what Jet had been, making nonsense of the obscure suspicions he'd been clinging to. It was she whose grief had made the act of violence by which Ross Pardee had died a vicious, animal deed for which there could be no excuse, bringing the knowledge home to Ben so strong that he was left sick and empty, with a need to drown the stinging bite of her words that echoed again now in his brain. . . .

"You never found where the boy was buried?" Matson pressed him.

He noticed Matson refilling his own glass, then glancing at Ben's to make sure it was still full.

"Your men buried him, I'm told," Ben said.

Matson frowned. "That's true enough, I reckon," he admitted. "But like I told you I wasn't there. I'm not just sure who was in on the buryin', but I'll find out. You can depend on me for that, Mr. Webber. Your boy worked for me, and I'm not a man to let one of my boys down."

"It doesn't matter."

"Now you're feelin' low," Matson said. "You'll see things different in the mornin'. Drink up, Mr. Webber."

Ben drank. He watched the glass fill up again. Matson was matching him glass for glass. He'd emptied his own and poured it full. Ben knew he was drinking too much and too fast, but a reckless indifference possessed him and a craving to build the fire high and fill that numb void inside. He listened for Julie's voice but couldn't hear it. Had she gone? Had she led some drunken cowboy up the stairs?

". . . no reason to doubt your word," Matson was saying. "But you've come a long way, Mr. Webber, just to turn around and ride back empty-handed. Now you'll have to admit that takes some convincing. If I were a suspicious man, I'd think you might have figured you stumbled onto somethin' and you didn't want it known."

Ben didn't answer. Why wouldn't the man believe him? No one had accepted the fact that he had come to Red Peak in peace, and now they wouldn't believe that he was leaving. A man who wouldn't take the straightness of another's words was often crooked with his own. The line of thought beckoned Ben, but the effort of following it didn't seem worth while.

With surprise he saw that his glass was brimming over when he thought he'd drained it. Musing, it came to him that Matson was deliberately trying to get him drunk. A distant bell of warning rang deep inside his brain, too thin and weak to make him listen to it. He felt no wonder, no anger. There was a devil prowling inside him now, trying to break out, a devil he'd thought long since broken and saddled and made peaceable. He saw Matson staring at him. The man raised his glass. Ben followed suit.

Time disappeared in the smoke and noise and confusion. The fire burned high, raging in his belly. Ben had to force his eyes to focus on the man across the table. It was like peering through the distortion of curving, smoky glass. The image wavered, smiling at him, smiling with a white gash of teeth, the silver hair at Matson's temples shining with a gloss like that on a sweating horse. There was a moment when Ben knew that he'd been tricked, that he'd let himself be taken for a fool, not allowing for the bitterness of mood that had combined with his empty belly to make the whisky hit him hard and fast. By then there was no turning back. The fire's flames licked at his brain.

Julie's face swam before his eyes. Her hand was tucked under his arm and she was trying to help him stand. "Come on, Ben. Come with me."

"No," he muttered thickly. Matson's blurred face leered at him. Why? he thought. Why get him drunk?

"You've had enough," Julie pleaded. "Please, Ben. Let me—"

"Upstairs?" Ben roared, lurching to his feet, "Is that it? Make him forget?"

"Ben!" The pain in her face reached through the flames. There was an instant's clarity in which he felt regret. It was not her doing. She had been Jet's girl. Jet's—

"Another drink, Mr. Webber?" Matson's voice was cool, insinuating.

"No!" The moment's sanity was gone. "With you? You pulled the trigger!"

Matson was on his feet. "What's that supposed to mean?"

"Don't, Ben! You don't know what you're sayin'!" Julie tugged at his arm. "Listen to me!"

And at last the devil broke out, the devil he'd hidden for so long, so many years, hidden from himself as he'd cloaked it before the world. He heard the laughter behind him, the shouts and jeers, and before him, arrogant and smiling, was Matson's face. The bottled hate and anger and bitterness exploded. With a single sweep of his hand Ben lifted the heavy table and flung it aside. Glasses skidded and smashed on the floor, and the table crashed onto its side. Ben lurched toward Matson, swinging at the grinning face. He felt the sharp bite of teeth as his fist smashed into Matson's mouth. A chair got in his way, tangling his feet. He stumbled, off balance, and half fell against another table which skidded under his weight. Still on his feet, Ben looked wildly for Matson. Another man moved toward him, another meaty face. Heavy hands grasped at him. Ben threw himself forward. His fist smacked solidly against flesh. The face was gone. Someone roared with rage nearby. A bottle crashed and something heavy fell. There was shouting now and the shrill screams of women. Two figures grappled in front of Ben as the fighting spread. He drove joyfully into the melee. A frantic rhythm jabbed at his senses. The piano! He broke loose from a choking arm and weaved toward the music. Someone fell against him. A fist came out of nowhere to thud against his jaw, spilling him backward, but there was no pain, no feeling. A foot came at him and he grabbed it, twisting, feeling the weight behind the foot lift and give, hearing the bellow of rage and pain. Then he was hit again and he was falling back, toppling, losing his balance and crashing against a solid, angular object. Chaotic music thundered in his ears. Before his eyes was a frightened, pinched face under a bowler hat. With a roar of satisfaction Ben picked up the pianist and swung him clear of the floor. "Please! Don't!" Ben threw him into the swarm of men.

He reeled against the piano. Looking down he saw the white keys gleaming like teeth. Grinning. Contemptuous and cunning grin. "Stop him!" a shout came. "He'll break the piano!" Ben reached for the circular stool. Hate's flame seared his brain. He raised the stool in his hands, bringing it high above his head. Smash it! Smash the grinning mouth!

"Stop him! Dammit! Don't let him!"

Someone dove into his belly, driving him back. Hands grabbed his upraised arms and pulled. "Throw him out!" There were many of them now, dragging him down, tearing the stool from his hands, smashing at him with fists and boots. He tasted blood. With unbridled fury he fought back, but the hands were too many. He was being carried, kicking and struggling, through a wild hubbub of sound, of shouts and curses and splintering wood and shattering glass as the drunken fights sparked by Ben's explosion still continued. The men carrying Ben charged through the swinging doors, using him like a battering-ram. Then he was under a spinning canopy of sky and he was in the air, arms flailing, until he thudded onto the hard dirt street to roll and tumble.

He lay there, breathing heavily through his open mouth, hearing the yells and taunts tossed at him from the boardwalk. He tried to rise and fell back. The noise of fighting in the saloon had dimmed. Ben struggled to his hands and knees. The ground bucked and pitched, trying to throw him. He held on. The saloon's lighted face circled dizzily around him. There were blurred figures and the rasp of mocking laughter. Ben shook his head and braced himself and staggered to his feet.

"Come out!" he roared. "One at a time! Matson! I know you're there! Come out and fight!"

Laughter. A derisive shout. Dizziness. The grinning devil stood before him, not Matson but his unleashed self. Ben groped for understanding but it fled before him. And in spite of all the drink the black hollow was still there in his belly, yawning and bottomless. With a growl of defiance he staggered away, feet dragging and stumbling in the dust of the street. A dumb purpose prodded him and guided his feet.

The stable loomed dark and quiet. Cautious now with a drunken cunning, Ben felt his way among the stalls until he found the mustang. A horse nearby whinnied in protest, and the mustang stamped his feet nervously. Ben clucked at him. His tongue was thick and clumsy. With fierce concentration Ben led the horse toward the pale rectangle of the door.

It took a long time for fumbling, awkward fingers to hitch the mustang to the rig. As if sensing the difference in him, the horse pulled away from him, skittering restlessly.

"Hold, boy," he muttered. "Hold. 'S all right. Just old Ben."

He leaned against the wagon until the sky began to wheel more slowly. For a moment he forgot his purpose, his mind as blind as sightless eyes. His weight shifted and he stared at the bottom of the wagon's deck. His fingers closed over the edge of the side panel. The rim of a coffin. That was it.

He began to search for a shovel. Stumbling back inside the stable he groped in the darkness, finding rope and harness first and a pile of blankets and a gap-toothed fork. Moving on, he tripped and fell. Mumbling in anger at his clumsiness, he crawled along on hands and knees next to the wall of the barn. His hand touched cold metal. He felt and traced the hard outline of a shovel's heel. Triumphantly on his feet he carried it to the rig. The mustang stood motionless, patient now and waiting.

Ben drove through a weird nightmare under an unsteady sky in which the stars rolled in slow circles and he swayed dangerously on the narrow seat. The grinding of the rig's wheels seemed deafening. He came around the brow of the hill and stopped. All was abruptly silent, and the stillness pounded in his head. He clambered down, gripping the shovel, and stood rocking on his feet, staring at the white slabs which projected from the ground below him like broken teeth. Which grave? What pile of earth covered the flesh and blood that had grown from his seed in Ellen's body?

Ben stumbled down the slope. There. The earth was fresh and dark and broken. Beneath it lay the killing fury, the wildness Ellen had tamed. A splinter of memory stabbed his brain. He saw a face, stove-red with anger, saw a big fist clubbing in the mindless joy of fighting, saw the man fly back from the impact that made his jaw a broken, hingeless thing—

No! Sweat stood out on his forehead. That had not been Jet. That had been *his* fist, *his* killing anger. Ben's! This was the wildness he had feared, the devil that lurked inside him whose specter he had seen in his son. For a moment Ben confronted the naked ugliness of a truth he'd hidden from himself, laying bare the guilt so long denied. He had killed in drunken brawling. And Ben remembered now and understood the hurt he'd seen in Ellen's eyes that morning when they found that Jet had gone. Ben had tried to destroy the image of his own wild temper seen in Jet. Instead he'd set it free. . . .

The shovel dug savagely into the earth. Ben worked in a kind of frenzy, digging, straining with back and arms to lift and throw, the sweat pouring down his face and sides. And then, as his foot slammed down on the shovel, it skidded off the steel grip. He was thrown off balance. His leg twisted under him and he fell.

Someone snickered.

Ben rolled on his back. Two shadows moved close, taking human shape. The thick one faced him while the other, slimmer figure sidled around behind.

"Lookin' for somethin', cowboy?"

Not Jake Howell then. But he knew that voice—

The man behind him laughed again. "I theenk he's

diggin' his own grave."

"Naw, he's plantin' flowers. How about that, tough man? Ain't that it? Ain't you plantin' flowers for that kid of your'n?"

With a choked cry of rage Ben lurched upward. Before he'd gained his feet a toe lashed at his ankle from the rear. He tripped, grabbing air, and the big man moved in fast from the front, his fist smashing into Ben's face. He sprawled full length on his side. The ground rocked under him.

Instinct made him roll away from the boot which swung at him. He heard the thick man grunt with effort as the kick missed. Scrambling erect, Ben saw the glint of red hair and the blurred outline of Red Morrell's thick features. He didn't have to look to know the other man was Chico. He had time to wonder if this was Matson's revenge for a broken mouth—or something more important, the need to still Ben's questioning voice.

Then Chico hit him in the back, driving him forward into Morrell's arcing fist. Ben's nose was ground against his face, queerly tingling. He swung low, his fist thudding into the big man's hard-muscled belly. Morrell gave ground. Not soft at all, Ben thought automatically, giving rebuttal to Indian Joe's estimate of Morrell. With a sweep of his arm, Ben flung Chico away from him. The wiry Mexican was on his feet again instantly, leaping forward. Ben shook his head to clear the cobwebs from it. They stayed in front of his eyes as he stalked Morrell and swung. The blow glanced off the gunman's cheek.

Chico landed on Ben's back like a cat, his legs tangling with Ben's, his arm snaking around Ben's throat, tightening against his windpipe. Ben clawed at the choking band. Morrell moved in, his boot smashing down on Ben's instep. Ben fought the pain and doubled over, trying to throw Chico off his back, but the movement left him open to the brutal thrust of Morrell's knee as he brought it up to crash against Ben's jaw.

He went down, Chico still hanging on his back. They rolled together. There was a roaring in Ben's ears. He gagged, struggling for air. His jaw felt loose and broken, and he remembered again the man he'd killed with his drink-propelled fists, remembered the broken jaw and the horror of shock and pain in the dying man's eyes. . . .

Ben dug back hard with his elbows, driving them into the ribs of the man who clung to him. Chico cried out. His fingers raked Ben's face, digging at his eyes. Ben twisted violently and wrenched free. He tried to push himself up. His head swam and his eyes refused to focus. The raw whisky had drugged his senses, slowed him so his arms felt heavy and there was no strength in his legs.

He was on his hands and knees when Red Morrell's boot exploded against the side of his head. Ben had been kicked once by a horse. It felt the same, as if all the bone had shattered into fragments under the tight skin of his skull. He was down, drowning in a sea of endless pain. Voices drifted to him, bodiless and distant.

"Now we'll teach you to get nosy, cowboy!"

"I keel him!"

They let him rise. It took him a long time. He stood at last, leaning like a tall tree in the wind. He swallowed blood and pawed with his hand at his eyes, trying to part the curtain that had fallen in front of them. He heard

Chico's snickering laughter and lunged toward it. A fist drove into his belly, doubling him over, and another slammed down into the back of his neck, clubbing him forward on his face.

He tried to push up, but his arms would no longer support his body. They kicked him then, methodically and cruelly, in head and shoulders and ribs and sides. Consciousness left him and floated back. At the last there was no pain, only the thud of impact, the involuntary jerking of his body, the sickness of failure, and blessed darkness closing in to smother him. . . .

Ten

Ben woke to a knowledge of brightness and the feel of clean, cool sheets against his naked body. He lay still in the white, sun-washed room with the white curtains across the windows, astonished as much by his nakedness as by the unfamiliar surroundings. He tried to sit up in the bed. The movement set up a clamor of pain in his head and body like a dozen blacksmiths pounding metal amidst showers of white-hot sparks. An involuntary groan broke through his cracked lips and he fell back.

Simultaneously he remembered his drunken spree in the Gold Nugget and the brutal fight in the graveyard. Humiliating though the knowledge of his beating was, it was the foolish, violent, senseless rage preceding it that made him groan again in bitter self-condemnation. He shied away from the memory and the truths it led him to.

Slowly and carefully he began to move his arms and legs, flexing toes and fingers. Each movement brought its vivid aches, but there were no broken bones. Sharp lances of pain drove into his chest when he breathed, and he prodded the area gently with his fingers. His ribs were encased in bandage. There were other dressings on arms and face and above one knee. He wondered if a rib was broken. His nose was sore and swollen large but the bone felt firm. Aside from that, he was badly bruised and shy of patches of skin but he was whole. The fact surprised him.

The beating had been another warning then, the final one. They hadn't meant to kill him. But how had he got in this bed? And where was it? Frowning, he tried to trap the elusive fragments of memory hiding in the hills of his mind. There had been a moment in the night when he became aware of the creak of wagon wheels and the jars that drove pain through him. And he had dim impressions of driving the rig, half blind and sprawling on the seat, not knowing where his half-conscious need was taking him. They'd dumped him in the rig, he reasoned, and left him in the desert. And somehow he had found the strength and animal instinct to set the horse on its way. But where had he come?

The door opened. Ben stared in growing bewilderment as a young woman walked across to the bed. Disbelief crowded in on him, but there was no mistaking the chestnut-brown hair, curling long down her neck, the clear hazel eyes, the slim, strong, youthful body. This time she wore a white shirt whose cloth had the soft quality that good linen gets after many washings, but the close-fitting jeans were the same.

"You're awake," she said matter-of-factly.

"I am," Ben mumbled in confusion.

"You're a hard man to kill, Mr. Webber," Nancy

Pardee said.

"If they'd wanted to kill me they would have."

She frowned. Her eyes were faintly puzzled as she looked steadily at him, as if she saw something she hadn't expected to find. She seemed about to speak and checked herself.

"Where would I be?" Ben asked.

"At my ranch," she said. "What was mine."

"How did I get here?"

"I'm not exactly sure," she said. "I don't see how you could have driven far in the condition I found you in, but—"

"I was alone?"

"Yes. I heard you comin'—you made a lot of noise. I would have shot at you, but you were already lyin' across the seat of your wagon." Her tone was cool, detached. "I thought you was dead."

"I'd been in a fight."

"I reckoned you had," she said dryly. "By the look of you, you didn't win."

"It's close to three hours' ride," Ben said slowly. "Maybe more at night. I can't figure how or why I'd get here. I reckon I didn't much know where I was goin'."

"You knew," Nancy Pardee said. An awkwardness colored her voice. "You talked some while I was tendin' to you."

Ben stared at her, astonished. And suddenly he was conscious of his nakedness under the bedcovers. His confusion deepened and he felt his face reddening. "*You* tended to me?"

"I don't know why else you'd be in my bed," she said a

little tartly.

"By yourself? I mean—"

"There was no one here when you come," she said, not looking at him now. "My foreman had taken the last of my horses over to the Bar NZ—that's just beyond the pass to the north—and he didn't get back till two in the mornin'. You were already in bed—that is, I'd already got you into the house and cleaned up some. I was leavin' today," she added with seeming irrelevance. "It's Matson's now—the ranch, I mean."

She had regained her air of detachment and spoke of what she'd done with a casual tone that suggested her actions were simply the normal help one human being might give to another in trouble. She'd dragged Ben from the rig by herself and somehow got him into the house, where she had cleaned, dressed and bandaged his wounds, made sure he had no broken bones, and put him in her bed. Her foreman, whose name was Bill Daley, had returned after she'd finished and Ben was asleep. The sight of the rig had brought him running to the house in alarm. Ben gathered without her saying so that the foreman had been none too pleased about what she'd done. The impression made him wonder in passing what had kept the man on at the ranch to the last when the other hands had quit. Looking at Nancy Pardee as she stood beside the bed with the sun at her back, making a kind of mist around her hair, he thought he knew.

"I'm much obliged to you, ma'am," he heard himself saying.

She moved her shoulders slightly in what was intended to be an indifferent shrug. "I couldn't leave you out there," she said. Her eyes met his again and he saw the puzzled question in them. "It was Matson's men you fought with."

"I was drunk," Ben said.

"Yes, I know. Was that the only reason?"

"No."

An awkward silence fell between them. Ben wondered what he had said to her in his semi-conscious state while she treated him. He thought he understood the compulsion which had guided him to return to her. It would be guilt, the shame he'd felt on the previous afternoon for the grief the name of Webber had meant to her. A man will do strange things when he's only half-conscious and driven by a sense of guilt. That would be why he came. That's all it could be.

"I should be lookin' at those cuts of yours," Nancy Pardee said at last.

Ben's fingers tightened on the bedcovers. "I reckon not," he said.

A smile quivered fleetingly at the corners of her mouth, making him sensible of how curving and expressive her lips were. He suddenly saw what was different in her from the grim woman he had met the day before. The bitter sorrow was still there beneath the surface, but it had been somehow softened. It was less personal. Looking at her closely, he thought he could sense the sympathy awakened in her when she found him bloody and battered outside her house in the middle of the night. That was a woman's way of acting. Ellen would have done the same.

"You sure are a sight," she said.

"I suppose."

"I reckon maybe I might have been wrong yesterday," she said, more stiffly. "I owe you an apology for what I said."

"It's only natural for you to think the way you did."

"I still can't figure why Matson would set his men on you."

"I been asking too many questions," Ben said.

"About what?"

"About your brother and my son and the way they died."

The friendliness that had seemed about to settle on her face moved away. "What's there to ask about?" she said, turning toward the window.

"I'd like to know what was behind the trouble between Matson and your brother. I've heard it explained, but I'd like to have you tell me the way you saw it."

Ben's own words surprised him. When he had left this very place the afternoon before all hope had died in him. He'd been ready to leave Red Peak, to give up even his mission of taking Jet's body back with him. He'd been convinced that all of his vague suspicions were without meaning or significance. Now everything was different. It was as if he'd been trying to peer through a mountain mist that hung low, obscuring things, until suddenly he'd ridden out of the mist into the sunlight where everything was sharp and clear. He saw himself, and there were things there to see that didn't tend to make a man comfortable with himself. He saw the deliberate intent in John Matson's trying to get him drunk and then having him jumped by Red and Chico, and this planned sequence made it clear that the beating had not been a momentary revenge for the brawl Ben had started in the saloon. Ben saw these and all the other obstacles that had been put in his way since he'd arrived in Red Peak, and he knew there was more to Jet's death than he had yet learned. This wasn't wishful thinking any more.

Nancy Pardee was speaking about Matson. "When he first come to town, takin' over the Gold Nugget, the men of the territory were glad to have him. He took a little, run-down place and dressed it up real nice, from what I hear. He had good whisky, gamblin', and"—she hesitated, glancing over her shoulder at Ben—"pretty girls. The ranchers hereabouts figured their boys needed a place in town to go to."

Ben nodded. "A man gets thirsty."

"Well, Matson did well. Better than anybody figured, I reckon. He started to buy up land. Then when we had two bad winters in a row and the drought last summer hit us all hard, some of the ranchers needed money to keep goin'. Matson was right friendly. He was glad to lend money."

"That's how Ross come to owe him?"

She stood with her back to him, staring out at the land that was now lost to her. "Not exactly," she said. She turned and her eyes were defensive. "Ross was a gambler, Mr. Webber. He thought he was better than he was, or maybe he trusted too much. I'm not sayin' for sure that Matson's card games are crooked, but Ross kept losin' steady. He lost a lot of money to Matson and he couldn't pay. Matson just laughed it off. He let Ross sign a note on the ranch just to make the loan legal. I didn't like it, but Ross wasn't worried. He figured it would be easy to pay off the note come fall."

Ben held still, letting her talk. That was a gambler's way of thinking, being optimistic, always figuring the next card up would be the good one, and betting with money you didn't have, trusting too much to luck. Pardee had played right into Matson's hands.

"It didn't work out that way," Nancy Pardee went on, her voice low and bitter. "We had a dry summer. When we couldn't pay, Matson was still right nice. He gave an extension till this spring. I guess he knew then we couldn't survive another hard winter."

Ben broke his silence. "There were others besides you and your brother?"

"Yes. One day we all woke up and found out Matson had grown a lot bigger than anybody had seen. He'd been buyin' more land, quiet-like. Then all of a sudden he wasn't smilin' any more when the notes come due. And he'd hired a bunch of gunmen in case some folks refused to pay or give up their land. He took over three other ranches, all in the valley here, before he got ours. One of the ranchers, Jesse Poulson, he went ridin' into town with a gun. He couldn't find Matson anywhere. Next time he went into town Matson was waitin' for him. They buried Jesse and one of his boys."

"Matson's hired guns killed them?"

"They got the one man. Matson drew on Jesse himself."

"I didn't figure him for a man to do his own killin'."

"Don't let him fool you, Mr. Webber. They say he's faster than any of the others. He just don't take any chances. He makes sure everything is stacked the way he wants it. The way Ross said it, when Matson calls you, you know he's got a pat hand."

Ben nodded, thoughtfully. She'd filled in some of the details he lacked—but he still didn't see just where Jet came in. Something was missing, something involving Ross Pardee and Jet. And there were other questions. . . .

"Where does the sheriff stand?" he asked. "With Matson?"

There was contempt in her flickering gesture of dismissal. "He hides behind the law. Some say he's killed a man or two in a fair fight, but I'd have to see it. One thing you can be sure of: if trouble starts, Jake Howell will be off somewhere else, and he'll have a lot of reasons why he had to be there."

"He didn't try to do anythin' about the men that Matson killed?"

She shook her head impatiently. Her brown hair moved heavily against her neck. "He claims Matson was within the law. He was defendin' himself. And maybe that's true enough in its way. Matson's a careful man, Mr. Webber. He could handle the sheriff if he had to, but he likes to do things legal. Or fix 'em so they look that way."

Ben shifted uncomfortably in the bed. He'd been holding himself tense with listening, straining to find some new fact in the story she told him. Movement made him painfully aware of the aches and bruises that covered his body.

"You said somethin' about your brother bein' a fighter, Miss Pardee. He didn't ride into town after Matson the way this other man did, this Poulson?"

"No. He talked of it, but I wouldn't let him. And he knew he wouldn't stand a chance."

Ben watched her closely, trying to clear the blurred portrait he had in his mind of Ross Pardee. You had to try to see behind the coloring of a sister's words. A real fighting man wouldn't let himself be talked out of a showdown with Matson. He wouldn't care about the odds.

"But he did try to fight, you said."

"His way." She'd caught the hint of doubt in Ben's question and her chin came up. She was the fighter, Ben thought admiringly. "Ross wasn't a man to give up easy. And he was a good talker, Mr. Webber. Not smooth like Matson, but he could make men listen to him when he had a thing to say. He argued that the small ranchers couldn't fight Matson alone but they could do it together. And if any one of them gave up or lost his land, that made the odds better for Matson. So Ross tried to organize the ranchers to get them to help each other. Maybe he was bein' selfish, because we were the ones needed help first, but what he argued made good sense. Some of the other ranchers thought so too. They bought up what stock we had left at a good price, and a few scraped up what money they could. That's why Ross was killed when he was, Mr. Webber—because he'd raised almost all of the money we needed to pay Matson off!"

Her voice rose sharply and broke. She swung abruptly away to hide her face, and Ben saw her shoulders quivering. Her last words had jarred him. They made the shooting of her brother, and the timing of it, look carefully planned. Once the ranchers had found they could beat Matson by teaming together, their opposition to him would have become stronger. They would have gained courage from Ross Pardee's actions if he'd been allowed to win. And maybe this was what Matson was trying to cover up now. If Ben probed too deep, maybe he wouldn't succeed in clearing Jet at all. A planned murder put Jet in an even blacker role. But Ben might dredge up evidence that would tie Matson in directly with the killing. That would be reason enough to try to frighten him off. All the pieces seemed to fit. And yet—

"I'd like to know exactly what happened the day of the shooting," Ben said. "I'm sorry to make you tell of it, but I have to know."

"It won't do you no good," she said. Her voice had a quaver in it but she had herself under control again. "Maybe you're different from your son, but that don't change what he was or what he did."

"Did your brother say anythin' about meetin' him? Had they had dealings of any kind you know of?"

She shook her head. "When he left—last Saturday it was—he wouldn't tell me where he was goin'. But he was in high spirits, laughin' and jokin'. Once or twice he hinted that Matson had a surprise comin' to him. I figured Ross had found someone who'd lend him the last of the money we needed to pay off the note, and Ross wanted to surprise me, too."

"Did he say where he was headin'?"

"No," Nancy Pardee said hesitantly. "But he must have gone straight to town. He left here late in the afternoon and he was seen with Webber just after sundown. That was just before it . . . it happened."

She was facing him now. The light and humor had all gone out of her face, and she stood a little farther away from the bed, as if her recounting of the events leading up to Ross Pardee's murder had sharply reminded her of the barrier that stood between her and Ben. He saw the change in her, the conscious withdrawal, and he was more aware than ever of the closeness that had almost come to them and of the strong attraction he felt toward this lonely, courageous woman. A day before this he had not known her, but now everything he saw in her—the fine curves of her body, the lift of her chin, the rich brown of her hair, the directness with which her eyes met his, the soft depression of her tan throat above the white shirt—all seemed warmly familiar, as if she had lived in his mind for a long time and he saw her with a series of faint shocks of recognition.

He had to force himself to speak. "Indian Joe testified he saw 'em," Ben said. "You know he can't see very good."

"That doesn't matter," she said emphatically. "Everyone knew Jet Webber and the way he dressed. It was easy to pick him out. And Joe sees well enough to recognize a man. Besides, he heard your boy call out to Ross."

"He knows more than he's told," Ben said slowly. "This mornin' I talked to him and we went to the graveyard. He couldn't find Jet's grave, though he says he buried him. Then he started to tell me somethin' more and somebody took a shot at him. After that he wouldn't talk."

Her eyes widened. "A shot? At Joe? I don't—" She stopped, frowning. "You sure that shot wasn't meant for you? It seems to me that you're the one that isn't very welcome here."

Ben was silent. It could be that the shot was just another warning to him, but he doubted it. Joe had been afraid. The shot had silenced him just on the point of talking.

"Joe wouldn't see a man hang unless he was sure," Nancy Pardee said, reading his thoughts.

"No," Ben agreed. And Joe's air of certainty couldn't be denied. Yet Ben was sure the old man's vision wasn't sharp enough to pick out a man's face at any distance in the tricky light of dusk. Would the black clothes that Jet had worn be enough to explain Joe's certainty? Ben sighed. If only he knew what the old man had been about to tell him. It was hard to believe that the whole town could have been wrong about Jet's being at the scene. And why would he be there trailing Pardee if not to use the gun he was hired for?

Reluctantly he turned his mind to another question. "Do you know who it was that hanged Jet?" he asked.

Nancy Pardee shook her head. "No one's talkin', and I wasn't there. I can't say for sure I wouldn't have been if I'd known in time."

Looking at her, Ben saw the stubborn set of her mouth and the proud way she stood, her gaze meeting his, level and defiant. Yet he knew her words were no more than words. She was a woman strong and brave enough to go after a man with a gun, but she wouldn't have been party to a lynching without trial. People often spoke out stronger than they meant when hurt or anger stirred them. What she said only showed that the time had passed when they could talk as a man and a woman sharing a brief moment of warmth and understanding. Each word he said now reminded her that Ben's son was her brother's murderer.

"I reckon I'd better be movin' on," he said gently. "If you'll let me dress."

"You can't get up! You shouldn't move so soon. I mean . . ." She let the objection die.

"I'll manage. But I want to thank you again for what you did for me. Weren't for you, I wouldn't be goin' anywhere this day."

"I'd have done the same for any critter I found hurt."

Her words, curt as they tried to be, failed in their purpose, for they only pointed to the need she felt to say them, to deny the personal feeling they both sensed.

"I reckon you would," he said.

She turned toward the door. Impulsively she whirled to face him again. "I know what you're tryin' to say," she cried. "You said it last night and other things that had best be forgotten. You won't believe your son's a killer. You're tryin' to say that he didn't do it, that somethin' else happened that night. But you're wrong, Ben Webber! It's no use! I don't know what Matson has against you, but nothing he does now—nothing you can do—will change what happened!"

Ben felt the pain behind her words and he was moved by it. But his mouth too was set in a grim and stubborn line.

"Maybe Jet did what they say," Ben said. "And you have reason to feel the way you do. I thought he did it myself yesterday. But now I'm not so sure—and I aim to find out."

Her expression altered slightly, and for a moment he thought he saw concern in her eyes. Then memory rose again and her lips tightened. "You'll only get yourself killed," she said tonelessly.

Ben looked at the space separating them, a distance made permanent by death, and he knew that she felt the same regret that stirred in him.

"If Matson figures he has to kill me," he said, "I reckon that'll prove somethin' one way or another."

Their eyes held for a moment longer. When she turned and left the room it was as if something had been wrenched loose deep inside him. A horse nickered outside, and the restless sound made the room seem more silent and empty.

Eleven

Bill Daley had a dark face dominated by thick black eyebrows and a black mustache that drooped at the ends, giving his mouth a turned-down expression. He had broad shoulders and a deep chest and thin, spindly, bowed legs that didn't look as if they could support his weight. He helped Ben load some bags and gear into the wagon after Ben offered the space, but he did it in sullen silence. Ben paid him little notice. He had enough on his mind mastering the stiff, sore muscles of his body and forcing them to do his bidding.

There was little talking up to the time they rode off. Nancy Pardee had suggested Ben might as well ride back to town with them if he felt fit. She said it as if it made no difference to her. When Ben was in the rig and ready he saw the woman standing apart, looking out over the valley, squinting against the sun that stood high overhead. Her gaze swung slowly, lingering often on some point that would have meaning only to her. At the last she stared at the ranch buildings silently. Ben followed her gaze. He wondered if she had been there when the logs of the house were set in place and the boards of the bunkhouse slapped together and the thin saplings cut for the tall frame of the corral. He wondered if she and her brother had done it together. The place had been kept neat and clean, with the bushes trimmed away around the buildings and a small garden carefully tended near the main house. But already, seeing the place with Nancy Pardee's eyes, Ben thought it showed an emptiness. Maybe it was the bare windows where the curtains had been taken down. Or maybe it was just the stillness of waiting.

She swung aboard her gelding and took its reins. Her face was bleak and her eyes were dry. She rode ahead without looking back. Bill Daley followed on a black horse, leading another that was laden down with baggage. Ben trailed in the rig.

The sun was hot on his back. He hoped it would bake some of the stiffness and soreness out of his muscles. After a while he could feel his feet warm and damp inside their boots and the sweat making his shirt cling to his back. The silence was broken only by the ringing clop and thud of hoof on rock or dirt, the creak of saddle leather, the snorting of the horses breathing dust, the slow churning of the wagon wheels.

They went through the north pass in file. When the land opened out beyond it in a broad shelf Ben saw the foreman knee his horse into a faster trot that brought him level with Nancy Pardee. They spoke but they were now too far ahead for Ben to catch the words. The man's eyes couldn't keep from flicking over the woman's body as they rode close together. Ben had to smile a little. It was easy to understand Bill Daley's glum look. If Ben was any judge at all, the foreman would have been working hard without making any progress, like an overeager bull caught in deep sand.

The smile flattened out as Ben remembered his own wild, drunken rage of the night before. It hadn't happened to him in a long time, so long he'd almost succeeded in shutting the knowledge of it out of his mind. He had not always been a man slow to anger. There had been a time when the wildness rode him instead of being ridden, not an angry violence but a senseless need to smash and break and hit when he was crossed or when drink loosened up the harness that society broke a man to wear. It was funny how a man could forget— or, if he remembered, find excuses for the way he was. He'd seen no harm in the rawness of his youth in a soldier's night of roarin' and brawlin', or in a cowboy's spree at the end of the trail. He'd even found excuse to ease the chafing of guilt when a man died before his fists.

It was Ellen who had learned to tame and direct the streak of wildness in the Webber blood, letting Ben discover the satisfaction of working anger out in sweat, the pride of knowing he was his own man to control. Perhaps because she had been his mother, she couldn't do the same for Jet.

And Ben had failed.

He closed his eyes and bent his head, remembering. The sun beat hot and red against his lids, and his eyes stung. A father saw the wildness different in his son. He didn't see that Ben's exultant fist smashing into weaker flesh was much the same as Jet's quick hand darting to draw and level and squeeze in killing anger. Maybe the one might have been shackled as the other had. And there might even have been another side to the story of that first shooting. He would never know. He'd never given the boy a chance to tell his side.

Ben Webber looked up and blinked. Heat waves made the narrow trail ahead shimmer, and the two figures on horseback undulated as they rode. The beating had taken a lot out of him, Ben thought. Maybe that's why his eyes were blurred. But he saw things clearer with his mind than before.

Twelve

The sun was still high when they rode into Red Peak early that afternoon. Coming in from the north end of town past the stable, Ben could see a crowd far ahead clustered in the middle of the street near the sheriff's office. He gave no more than a passing wonder to this unusual activity for the heat of the day, until he saw a man look toward him, point and shout. Another cowboy down the line took up the cry and, turning, ran awkwardly on his high-heeled boots toward the knot of men in the street. Nancy Pardee and Bill Daley rode ahead of Ben. A man called something out to them from the boardwalk and they both turned in their saddles to stare back at Ben.

Curiosity tugged at him. He'd broken a table or two in Matson's place during the brawling, but that would hardly account for the excitement his appearance was causing. There was something ominous and threatening about the way the crowd swung to watch him approach, some of them spreading out, unconsciously making a perfect circle into which Ben drove the rig and stopped. It was only then that he saw Jake Howell standing on the walk in front of his office.

"That's him, the murderin' sidewinder," someone snarled.

"Nerve of him, drivin' right in like that."

The sheriff stepped down into the dust of the street. The big .45 in his hand was trained on Ben's chest. He looked unhappy.

"Ben Webber?" he called loudly, as if he were asking a question.

Ben held still, watching the sheriff and at the same time taking in the threatening movement of the crowd as it closed in to surround him and the wagon. Nancy Pardee and Bill Daley still sat their horses not more than spitting distance away, themselves caught in the circle of the crowd. There was a puzzled question in Nancy's eyes as she stared hard at Ben.

"I'm placin' you under arrest," Jake Howell said.

Ben felt a tension of waiting in his body. "What for?" he asked quietly.

"Listen to him!" a voice cried from the crowd. "He'll try to worm out of it."

"Don't let him bluff you, Sheriff!"

"You know damn well what for," Howell blustered threateningly. "For the killin' of Injun Joe!"

Stunned, Ben could only stare at him.

"You jest saved us a lot of trouble," the sheriff went on. "I was organizin' a posse to track you down. I warned you, Webber, not to go stirrin' up trouble in this town."

Ben's eyes met Nancy Pardee's. "I didn't do it," he said flatly.

"No use tryin' to deny it." Jake Howell squinted up at Ben, his little eyes almost lost behind the puffy, bunched-up lids. "We got you cold."

Ben thought of the gnarled old Indian scout, clinging desperately to the pride of his past, and a flame began to burn at the base of his skull. He held it, controlling it, pushing it back when its fingers tried to lick through his brain. There came a time when a man must live or die according to the depth to which he had plumbed himself and the degree to which he could use the good and bad he'd found without letting it use him. Ben knew he'd reached that time. He had to keep himself cold and clear of mind, the violence in him under check.

"I never killed Joe," he repeated.

"Sure, that's what he'd say," a man shouted. "What d'you expect?"

Suddenly Luke Harris was pushing through the crowd beside the wagon, his right arm held in a sling, his yellow eyes baleful with hate. "I made a coffin for Joe," he yelled. "I can make one for his killer, too!"

"We took care of one Webber. We know how to deal with this one!" someone answered him.

"String him up!"

The cry went up, echoed by a scattering of voices, then sweeping through the crowd like a prairie fire. There were troublemakers there, Ben thought, trying to stir up the others, but there were still many who waited, uncertain of their anger or Ben's guilt.

"Just a minute!"

The cool voice cut through the rising rumble with a sharpness of authority that made heads turn quickly and stilled the cry for action. Nancy Pardee sat erect on her gelding, above and aloof from the crowd. Jake Howell looked up at her and mopped his brow with the back of his hand.

"Suppose you tell us what happened to Joe," she said coolly, "before there's talk of another hangin'."

"Now you'd best keep out of this, Miss Nancy," the sheriff said. "It's nothin' to do with you."

"Maybe not. You all know I've no cause to call this man a friend. But any man deserves to know what he's accused of."

There was grumbling among those nearby who heard her words. Luke Harris put a bony hand on the rig. "Let's tell him with a rope!" he urged.

"Now hold on there!" Jake Howell pleaded. "Maybe Miss Pardee's right. No harm in—"

"We're wasting time! Get him!"

Ben sat quietly, unmoving, acutely conscious of the fact that he was unarmed and virtually helpless to resist the mob. He looked admiringly at Nancy Pardee, sitting so calm and straight in the saddle, making no move to push clear of the milling mob of men.

"Hold it!" Ben's head jerked quickly toward the board-walk as he recognized John Matson's voice. Matson stood at the edge of the walk, two steps up from the street and looking over the heads of the crowd. There was something meaningful in the way he stood higher than the others, free of the dust of the road, even his clothes setting him apart— the costly gray coat over the checked vest, the expensive gray Stetson meeting his silvery temples. "Let the sheriff have his say," Matson argued, contempt in his tone. "Let Webber know why he can't wriggle out of this. We've got plenty of time for a necktie party."

"He's right and that's a fact," Jake Howell shouted. "Now let's calm down here and let me talk."

"You talk too much, Jake," someone called good-naturedly.

Howell glared in the direction of the offending voice, his black beard jutting out. "I want order here," he declared aggressively, "and that's for damned sure!" He swung back toward Ben, whose eyes had picked out Red Morrell and

Chico close to Matson on the boardwalk, leaning against a post. Chico grinned at him. One of Morrell's eyes was puffed up, and there was venom in the other eye.

"Now don't try to interrupt me, Webber," the sheriff said. "You'll have time to say your piece when I've finished."

"Cut the palaver," Luke Harris said nastily.

Howell's beard quivered with indignation, but he went on. "Old Joe come into the Gold Nugget lookin' for you last night, Webber. That was after you'd got drunk and tried to smash up the place and got thrown out. Guess Joe'd got hold of a bottle somewheres hisself, 'cause folks say he was in his usual condition. Don't know where he's been gettin' all his whisky money lately, but he has."

There were no guffaws. The crowd was silent now, listening, watching Ben's face.

"Did he say why he wanted me?" Ben asked.

"Now you hold still," Howell said, glaring. "Nobody knows why he wanted you—'cept you, that is—but he come askin' for you and that's enough. Mr. Matson here, he told Joe you'd been thrown out. Then Dale Prouther told Joe he'd seen you around the stable earlier. That right, Dale?"

A man Ben didn't know pushed through the crowd close to the sheriff. "Yessirree, that's it, Sheriff. I seen him there for sure. Huntin' for somethin', I think he was, out behind the stable. And I told old Joe that's where I seen him."

The crowd's silence now had tension in it, as if the mention of Indian Joe's name had centered their attention on the reason for being here. Ben waited, listening close, knowing this was the only trial he would ever get.

"There were a dozen witnesses or more," Jake Howell

said pompously, "so there's no use denyin' anythin', Webber. Injun Joe went lookin' for you and we know where he found you! You went diggin' in the graveyard, that's what, doin' jest what I warned you not to do. Joe found you there and you killed him!"

The men in the street began to mutter threateningly. Here and there a cry went up again. "Get a rope!" "String the bastard up!" The men nearest the wagon pushed against it, crowding close.

"What makes you think I'd kill him?" Ben asked. "I'd no reason."

"You were talkin' to him yesterday mornin'," the sheriff retorted. "How do we know what went between you? Anyways, from what I hear you didn't need no reason, not the way you was actin'. You like to took John Matson's place apart until folks had had enough of it and threw you out in the street."

There was a moment's silence. The crowd watched Ben, whose mind probed angrily at the problem of Joe's death. Why had Joe been looking for him? Was there something important that the old man knew, so vital that he had needed the false courage lent by drink to tell it, so damning that his tongue had to be stilled when he gave himself away in hunting for Ben at the Gold Nugget?

Had he lied about Pardee's murder after all?

"I've got a rope," a voice called sharply. It was Red Morrell, holding a coiled length of rope in his hand, raising it high so everyone could see it.

"You haven't offered proof enough to hang a man," Nancy Pardee spoke up again.

Jake Howell drew himself up as tall as he could. There

was triumph in his voice. "I'm the law here, Miss Pardee," he said. "And I know all about evidence. We've got all we need. Joe was shot in the head and chest. He was found this mornin' in the graveyard. Right nearby was the shovel Ben Webber stole from the stable last night and used to dig with. That'd be enough, but I've got more proof than that." He swung around and peered toward his office. A long-faced waddie stood in the doorway. "You got it there, Slim?" Howell called.

"I got it, Sheriff."

The lean man disappeared inside the office for a moment. When he reappeared he carried a rifle in his hand.

"Hold it up," the sheriff commanded. He raised his voice so everyone in the listening crowd could hear. "That there rifle was found nearby where Joe was lyin'. I guess if the man who used it on Joe had been sober he'd never of left it there to be found. But we all know Ben Webber was drunk." Howell spun toward Ben. "That your Winchester, Webber?"

Ben didn't need to have the gun in his hands to know that it was his. The plot was clear now. Joe had come to the wrong place looking for him. Killing the old man had been necessary, but with Ben already out of the way for the night, it had been easy to fix things to look as if Ben had shot Joe. No denial of his would be believed now. And his story of being attacked and beaten up would only be given the lie.

"Let me see the rifle," Ben said.

"Don't do it, Sheriff!"

"He don't need to see it!" Luke Harris snarled. "It's his all right. You can see that in his face!"

111

"It looks like mine," Ben admitted. "But I never used it last night. And aren't you forgettin' somethin', Sheriff? Someone shot at Joe and me yesterday mornin'. I told you about it."

"I'm not forgettin'. But there's only your word that shot was ever fired! No one else heard it, and Joe never talked about it to anybody. Looks like maybe you was jest settin' yourself up an alibi, like you was intendin' to shoot Joe all along and it wasn't jest 'cause you was drunk!"

The accusation was damning. The crowd's rumble grew louder. There was a stirring of movement toward the wagon. Someone tried to grab the rope from Red Morrell's hand. Ben saw Matson smiling at him from the boardwalk. The twist of his swollen lips held malice. The street was jammed now. The crowd had grown during the talk, drawn by Ben's arrival and the noise that followed. There were even womenfolk at the edges of the mob and farther along the street, trying to keep children away from the center of excitement. Near the swinging doors of the Gold Nugget across the street Julie Larkin stood, a blue shawl wrapped around her shoulders. Her face looked pale and worried.

"What time did this happen?" Nancy Pardee said suddenly to the sheriff, raising her voice to make herself heard.

"How do we know when the shootin' happened?" someone shouted.

"You know when Joe came lookin' for Webber!" she retorted.

"No offense, ma'am," John Matson called out, "but it 'pears to me you're takin' a powerful interest in savin' this man's neck, 'specially considerin' who he is."

Nancy Pardee's lips tightened, but her gaze didn't waver

from the sheriff. "What time was this?" she repeated.

Frowning, Howell swung toward the man named Dale Prouther who'd seen Ben near the stable. "Well?" the sheriff snapped. "What time was it you seen Webber?"

"Well, now, that was near ten or thereabouts," the man drawled. "Can't say exactly, but I know it was around ten."

"And when did you talk to Joe? What time was it he come to the saloon?"

"That I know," Prouther said emphatically. " 'Twas after midnight. Matson can tell you that."

The crowd had grown quiet, sensing importance not yet understood in these questions. Eyes swung toward Matson.

"Maybe it was midnight," Matson said. The smile had left his face. "I wasn't keepin' track. And I don't see that it makes any difference."

"Sure it was after midnight," Dale Prouther argued doggedly. "I asked you the time once myself, I remember, an' you had to take out that gold watch of yours. That was before Joe came, and it was close to midnight when I asked the time."

Jake Howell broke in impatiently. "I think Mr. Matson's right," he declared, looking uncomfortably at Nancy Pardee. "Can't see as it makes much difference when Joe was last seen. Webber could still have been in the grave-yard—"

"It makes a heap of difference," the woman said quietly. Her eyes met Ben's. "If Joe was killed after midnight, Mr. Webber couldn't have done it. He wasn't at the graveyard then. He was with me."

Her quiet words couldn't be heard very far. Among those near enough to hear, there was a stunned moment of silence. Then the news could be heard spreading through the crowd along the street.

Jake Howell's mouth gaped open. "With you?"

"He rode up last night. Must have been about one o'clock when I found him outside the house. He'd been in a fight and—and he was far gone with drinkin'. I took him in and cared for him." She paused to let her words sink in, then added, "It's a good long ride to my place. Even on a fast horse he couldn't have ridden it in an hour. And he came in a wagon."

The sheriff pivoted back to Ben. Confusion and uncertainty mingled in his face. "That true?" he demanded.

Ben nodded. He glanced up at the boardwalk. Red Morrell was watching him narrowly. Chico, still grinning, was fingering the edge of a knife blade, absorbed in it, seemingly oblivious of the excitement in the street. Now was the time to tell of the two men jumping him, Ben thought. Now he might be believed. But he said nothing.

"She's lyin'," Luke Harris growled angrily. "She must be!"

"Now hold your tongue!" Jake Howell swung on him. "We all know Miss Pardee, and we know she's no reason to be lyin' for him!"

Harris looked suddenly past him at Bill Daley. "Ask him!" he snarled. "He'll know if she's tellin' the truth!"

Ben had forgotten the foreman. He looked at him now. Daley had evidently been trying to stay close to Nancy Pardee, but the crowd had edged between his horse and hers, pushing them apart. His eyes peered out under their bushy brows at Ben with antagonism.

"He was there all right," Daley growled. "I can't say jest

when he come. I'd took some horses over to the NZ spread. When I got back this fella was already there."

"What time was that?" the sheriff asked.

"Two, maybe." Daley glared angrily at Nancy Pardee, and suddenly he blurted, "She'd put him in her bed. Said he was hurt, though it looked to me like he was jest drunk. They were there together in the house all night."

There was a change in the crowd's mood now. The silence grew awkward. Ben saw the damage in the way the foreman had made his statement—damage not to him but to the woman who had saved his life with her cool, quick thinking. Men stared curiously at her and looked quickly away. Her defense of him and the help she'd given him in the night were now twisted into an ugly thing. Ben had been taken into her house, had spent the night with her, in her bed—the man whose son had killed her brother.

"Well, now," Jake Howell said. "I guess maybe that changes things. If you say he was with you near one o'clock—"

"He was." Nancy Pardee's chin came up, proud and stubborn.

"I should still lock you up!" Howell declared, peering narrowly at Ben. "I warned you about diggin' up the grave—"

"Aw, forget it, Sheriff," a man spoke from the crowd. "We was wrong."

The sheriff glared, frustrated, unsure of himself. "I'll let it go this time," he blustered. "But you get no more warnings, Webber. Maybe you didn't kill Injun Joe, but you had somethin' to do with his gettin' killed, the way you been stirrin' things up. Leave things be, you hear?"

Ben looked at him coldly. "Maybe you'd better find out who did kill Joe," he suggested. "Or isn't that important any more?"

Baffled, Howell pawed his beard, fumbling for a retort. Abruptly he turned and bulled his way toward the steps leading to his office. The crowd began to move away, breaking up into groups, gradually dispersing down the street and into the saloon and along the boardwalk. Men talked low, with sheepish looks, or joked with the exaggerated loudness of embarrassment.

Ben's eyes met Nancy's. He stepped down from the rig and walked over to her. "I owe you another obligation," he said. "More than I reckon I can pay."

"You owe me nothing," she said stiffly.

"You'd have done the same for any critter?" Ben asked gently, smiling.

"I would," she snapped. "You needn't think there was anythin' personal in it, Ben Webber! I wouldn't see any man hang for somethin' he didn't do. And I don't care what folks think of me and what I do, either, so you have no call to be concerned about that."

"I am, though," Ben said, sober now.

"I'll look after my own reputation."

She started to rein her horse around, but Ben reached to stop her. "What about Joe's bein' killed?" he asked. "He wanted to tell me somethin'—and he was the only witness to your brother's death. Why do you suppose Joe was shot, Miss Pardee?"

She stared at him, and for a moment there was a startled wonder in her eyes. Then it was gone, and her lips tightened. "You're still tryin' to prove somethin' you can't prove," she said. "What will it show, Mr. Webber, when you get yourself killed!"

While the words still rang in Ben's ears, she kneed the gelding into motion and galloped down the street, her back held straight, head high. Even the horse's long tail, carried stiffly erect, seemed to be a sign of her proud denial of her feelings.

Ben turned from the sight of Nancy Pardee's retreating back to find another woman's eyes on him. For a moment his attention was arrested by the expression on Julie Larkin's face—a look that mirrored hurt and bewilderment. Standing slim and small on the busy boardwalk, she contrived somehow to seem forlorn and alone.

She tore her gaze away from his and hurried along the walk away from him, breaking into a trot, half stumbling once, as if she were running blindly away from misery she couldn't face. Ben stood rooted in the street, suddenly remembering the implication Bill Daley had tried to give his night in Nancy Pardee's house, knowing that Julie had taken the man's meaning and believed it. There was no mistaking the pain he'd seen in Julie's face. It was a woman's accusation of betrayal.

Angrily Ben searched the street for sign of Daley. The foreman was nowhere in sight. Having tried to do what harm he could, avenging himself on the woman who'd rejected him, he'd quickly disappeared. It wasn't likely he'd make himself too public for a while, Ben thought, savagely scuffing dirt with his heels as he walked back to the rig. A man who'd fight a woman with small words wasn't the kind who'd wait to face a man's answer.

Ben was in the act of swinging stiffly up to the wagon's

seat when he heard snickering laughter. In a flashing instant his memory tracked down the tantalizing familiarity of the mocking sound, and he knew before he looked that he would see the white-toothed grin of Chico. Something as hot and thick as boiling coffee bubbled up in him. Blood rushed to his face. He vaulted down to the street, body tensing in a crouch as he hit.

And there he froze. His mood cried out for the shock of violent contact. Every fiber of his body was taut with the need of it. All the frustration of two days of blind and fruitless searching focused now on the two men watching him, two men whose boots had left their marks all over his body, raw and red.

"You look mad, cowboy," Red Morrell called tauntingly. "Who you mad at?"

And Ben forced the clawing tension of his fingers to relax, forced his arms to drop limp at his sides, compelled himself to stand erect and to swallow the hot, bubbling rage and hold it down. He stared at the grinning, contemptuous faces and he did the hardest thing he had ever done in his life: he turned his back on them and climbed into the rig.

"Hey, did you see that, Chico? Now why do you suppose a man'd do that?"

Laughter, high-pitched as a woman's. Ben took the reins in his hands. The skin felt tight and pinched on his face, the way it feels when you've been out in the bitter cold of a winter storm and come suddenly into a room warmed by a blazing fire. He clucked at the mustang and flicked the reins.

"You know what he looked like to me, Chico?" Morrell drawled. "He looked scared! Now why do you suppose he was scared, huh?"

Ben swung the rig around in a half circle and started back up the street. The mocking, giggling laughter followed him.

"Look at him run, Chico! Look at him go!"

Ben found that his hands were trembling. He waited till the sound of laughter had died behind him, lost in the grating of the wheels and the familiar noises of the street. Then he let out his breath slow and easy. Tension still gripped his body, but as it began to ease and the mind he'd locked against thought broke into motion, he found within himself a strange relief. He had faced the naked wildness and he'd beaten it. That much he'd had to know. The other needs of pride could wait.

So could the reckoning.

Thirteen

He left the rig beside the livery stable and unhitched the mustang. A boy Ben had never seen before came out, all bony and gangling in that state of growth where a boy has no meat on him. He was awkward and nervous and tongue-tied as well.

"I'd turn him loose in the corral to cool before I'd water him," Ben said, handing the reins over to the boy with an air of casual confidence.

The lad nodded vigorously. "Yessir!"

Eagerly he led the horse away. On some kids the good stuck out all over, Ben thought, as prominent as this boy's mop of hair which had the color of a rusty nail. They jumped to a man's word, as anxious to please as a young widow. They were like a horse bred in the corral which took naturally to working with a man. If they had a colt's untamed streak, it was more playful than vicious and the years soon wore it out.

Ben turned away. He ladled a long cool drink from the bucket hanging from a rope in the well. The water gurgled in his belly. It came to him that Indian Joe had soon been replaced and would just as quickly be forgotten. They would bury him this day with a lot of pious thoughts, and they had been riled enough by his death so they'd come close to hanging Ben for it, but by tomorrow the mind would already be beginning to forget. A man even forgot a woman who'd been part of him for twenty years.

Of a sudden Ben had a clear, cold vision of the grizzled old scout stumbling through the darkness in search of him, full of drunken guilt and the need to unburden it. He'd never had a chance. What Joe had meant to tell him Ben might never know, but he knew it had been important. Ben was sure of that as he stared at the hill beyond which lay the graveyard where the old man had felt his way with groping hands held out before him, his eyes a blur, the whisky raw in his belly and sending fumes to cloud his brain. What would he have found waiting for him there in the shadow of the cottonwood at the foot of the hill? A dim shape he would have mistaken for Ben. Then, all at once, an orange spurt of flame, the crack of doom, a leaden weight tearing him apart, cutting off the protest that frothed at his lips.

His killer must feel proud.

Bleak-eyed, Ben Webber walked slowly back along the dusty street. It was nearly empty now in the heat of early afternoon. Morrell and Chico, Matson and the others, all had sought cool refuge out of the sun. Ben's boots stirred up dust which settled slowly behind him. Overhead, towering above the town, the mass of Red Peak glowed dull red.

He stopped at the sheriff's office. Howell, looking more surly than ever and wiping his sweating forehead with a big red handkerchief, swung half around in his swivel chair and avoided meeting Ben's eyes.

"I'll have my gun," Ben said.

"Don't know as I ought to let you have it," the sheriff complained. "Now don't go gettin' riled. I'm jest thinkin' of savin' your hide."

"I'll only use it to shoot snakes," Ben said with emphasis, and he waited.

Howell shifted his bulk uncomfortably, making the chair squeak. He nodded at his long-faced deputy, who sat in a straight chair tilted back against the wall. "Give it to him, Slim," the sheriff grunted.

Ben took the Winchester from the deputy. "You think this gun killed him?" he asked.

"Can't say for sure," Howell said. "Looked like it, and the gun had been fired."

"Kind of appears like whoever done it wanted it to look like I killed him," Ben suggested quietly.

"Now don't go jumpin' to conclusions," the sheriff protested. "You don't know that. And you don't know who shot Injun Joe!"

Ben held his tongue. No point in spilling everything he knew or thought before the sheriff and his deputy. "When's the buryin'?" Ben asked.

The abrupt shift of thought took the sheriff a moment to adjust to. "This afternoon. Harris is havin' the coffin made now. He can't do it hisself yet," he added pointedly, his small eyes peering narrowly at Ben. "You stayin' here?"

Ben weighed his answer. "For the funeral," he said. As he went out he felt an angry satisfaction at the disconcerted frown his answer left on Howell's face.

He stopped at the restaurant and ate in dogged silence, ignoring the stares of other men along the counter. It was hot and quiet in the room. Ben thought of the pancakes and syrup and coffee that Nancy Pardee had set out for him that morning after he'd dressed. That too had been a silent meal. She'd busied herself about the kitchen while he ate, presenting her back to him most of the time. The action had had the wrong effect, only making him conscious of the way she moved and how her brown hair curled heavy against her neck, making him remember with reddening face that she had dragged him in and undressed him and wrapped him up in bandage like a mother tending to a child, leading him to wonder what it might have been like to know this woman without a bitter barrier between them.

Out again in the dusty, deserted street, Ben walked slowly toward the hotel. One sound rang harsh in the quiet day, the methodical banging of a hammer driving nails into wood. You could hear an echo of the banging repeating it far off. The steady hammering followed Ben into the hotel and up the stairs. All over town men would be listening to it, waiting with a kind of tension for it to end. Even in a town like Red Peak men never got used to death.

The hall floor squealed under his foot. He came to his room and pushed the door open. His nostrils quivered with the sweet, remembered scent that Julie Larkin wore, even before his sun-blind eyes could find her across the room.

Fourteen

"I—I been waitin' for you."

"I see."

"I looked for you last night after they—after you left the Nugget." Suddenly the hesitant words spilled out in a rush like water breaking through a crack in a dam. "When I couldn't find you I was scared. I didn't know where you'd gone. I was afraid you'd been hurt. You were like a wild man, and I thought—"

The dam closed up, sealing off the torrent of words. In the stillness that followed the distant hammering could still be heard. Ben became conscious of the open door at his back. He shut it and faced the girl again. She stood near the window, her pale blue shirt carelessly open at the throat, adding its provocativeness to that of the long dark blue skirt whose soft fullness merely served to emphasize her slim waist and rounding figure. At the hurt he saw in her eyes Ben felt compassion move him.

"I heard where you were," she said in a small voice.

"What did you hear?"

Her eyes avoided his. "That you were with her. That she took you in and—and you spent the night with her."

"She did," he said. "She took me in."

There was a moment's pause. "You must have gone straight there," she said at length. "I guess where a man goes when he's not himself proves somethin'."

"When he's drunk, you mean?" There was no edge to Ben's correction, only a need to set things straight. "It can prove a lot of things, Miss Julie, or maybe nothin' at all."

"But you went—"

"I didn't go there right off. There was time for two of Matson's hands to jump me first. They drove me out in the desert in the wagon and left me there for the buzzards."

"Matson's men!"

"Red and Chico."

"But you never said anythin' to the sheriff! I mean—"

"You think they'd have admitted it? They had me all set for a rope."

"Mr. Matson wouldn't do a thing like that!"

Ben didn't answer her. Maybe she believed what she said, though it was hard to think that she could work so close to Matson and not know what he was.

"He wouldn't, unless—unless it was because you hit him. You cut his mouth bad and broke things up in the saloon. He was right mad at that."

"You think that was why Indian Joe was shot, too?"

"You can't blame that on Matson! Why would he want Joe dead?"

"I'm not sure—except that Joe wanted to find me and tell me somethin'."

She stared at him, anxiety in her face. Her small hands were clenched and twisting nervously, and there was a tiny crease of perplexity above her eyes. Ben was silent, letting her think it out. He took off his hat and hung it on a knob of the hard-backed chair. Julie's eyes widened, fixed on the bandage which had been mostly hidden by the crown of his hat.

"Ben! You *are* hurt!"

He shrugged. "Bruised some."

"That's really why she took you in! Not jest because

you—oh, Ben, I didn't know!"

He looked at her and then she was whirling across the room to fling herself against him, her arms tightening around his chest. Ben winced.

"Ben, honey, I—oh! I'm painin' you!"

He managed to grin down at her. "I ain't used to bein' squeezed so hard," he said gently.

She tilted her head up and the huge brown eyes filled with tears. Her face seemed to crumple like a child's, and the salt tears flowed down over the bright pink of her cheeks.

"You—you was hurt bad and I never knew it. I thought . . . Ben, honey!"

She dug her face into his chest, hiding it. Small fists clenched, tugging at his shirt sleeves. He could feel the swelling warmth of her tight against him, quivering with each muffled sob. A curious mixture of emotions left him rigid, his arms held down at his sides. The scent of flowers was in her hair and heady in his nostrils. He felt a quickening pity and tenderness that made him want to put his hands on her shoulders and hold her close. And he couldn't deny the pride that a woman so young and pretty could feel so strong about him. Hot coals burned where the ashes had long been cold, and he knew again a man's need of a woman. But with the compassion and the sudden desire there was a strange reluctance that held him still, a halter made of remembered guilt and an unexplained reserve, as if his mind was not as sure of her as his body was.

"I know what you're thinkin'," she said, raising her tear-streaked face. "But I wasn't really in love with Jet. We liked each other and he wanted to marry me. That was good enough for me. It was more than I could expect of a man. But it wasn't like this, Ben. Maybe I saw somethin' of you in him, just a part, without knowin' what it was I saw. But now I see it whole. In you, Ben! Don't you see what I mean? Do you know what I'm sayin'?"

"I reckon I do," Ben said thickly.

"I love you, honey! You got to believe me. I never felt this way before—not about any man. Not any!"

A quiet settled in him, a wary stillness. He was a man slow to say what he felt, suspicious of words that came too easy. She sensed the lack of response and drew back quickly. Her eyes searched his face.

"It ain't Jet," she said in a low voice. "It ain't him, is it? It's what I am. Ain't that it, Ben? You can't forget what I've been. That's what all men think, 'ceptin' Jet. She's just a—"

"No!" Ben said harshly. "I don't think that at all!"

"Then what? What is it, honey?"

He couldn't tell her. He couldn't say that he felt only an animal's need and a man's pity. That wasn't what she wanted. He couldn't say that a love that comes quick to the lips usually doesn't go much deeper or last much longer than the tellin'. He couldn't say that after his time with Nancy Pardee—or maybe it was just the way he'd seen himself so clear this morning—now he saw Julie different.

Unexpectedly he remembered the first woman he'd ever had. A green soldier he'd been, still wet behind the ears, not yet twenty-one, stuck-up proud of his brand new uniform and out to prove himself a man, trying to hide the way his hands shook and the panic that gripped his chest. That had been at Fannie's place, and the woman had picked Ben, he hadn't picked her. He was so scared that if he hadn't poured whisky down he'd never have been able to do it. Afterward she'd told him how good he was, how it wasn't that good for her with smaller men, and he was so full of himself he'd paid her extra. He remembered how she looked to him that night, all pink and pretty.

He'd sneaked around next morning to see if he could catch sight of her. She had come out the back way, and he hadn't recognized her until she spoke cheerily to him. In the stark light of morning her face was pasty white and her hair hung down in strings and the lines around her eyes and mouth made her out to be old enough to be his mother.

Was it like that with Julie, just seeing what she was in the cold light of day? Was it only what she thought it was, an instinctive rejection of her past? Ben shook his head. No. It was just that something was wrong, like a note of music that jars your ear even though you haven't the knowledge needed to pick it out or say just why it's wrong.

"You don't have to say nothin'," Julie said, all the life gone out of her voice.

"I reckon I do," Ben said. "You're wrong, Julie. I'm not judgin' you. Maybe it's just that until I do the job I come for, I can't let anythin' else happen."

"Oh, Ben, Ben honey, let it be! Get out of here! Even if I can't have you—even if it's too late for that—I couldn't bear it if you got hurt more. I don't understand all this, I don't know what's happenin', but I do know if you keep pressin' this thing about findin' Jet somethin' else will happen. Please, honey!" She came to him again and her fingers dug hard into his arms. "I'm beggin' you, Ben. Leave now!"

He took her hands and held them gently in his own. "I

can't," he said. "Too much has happened. Yesterday I might have. I told you so. I told Matson, too, but I reckon he didn't believe me. Things have gone too far now. Joe is dead. They tried to blame me for his killin'. It isn't just findin' Jet any more." Ben took a deep breath. "That's where it begins, and maybe that's where it'll all end, too, when I find him."

For a moment she looked at him. "You won't quit, will you? I reckon that's the kind of man you are, and if you were any different I wouldn't love you so."

She pulled free of his hands and walked over to the window, where she stood peering out at the street. Ben became aware of a total stillness. It took him a moment to realize why he was so conscious of the silence. The hammering had ceased.

"What will you do now?" Julie asked.

"I'll wait for dark," Ben said, "and get me a shovel."

"Have you found anythin'?" The question came out casual, but Ben sensed the interest in it. "I mean, do you know where Jet was buried?"

Ben hesitated. The wariness was even sharper, a tightening in his chest. Her curiosity was natural—but not the attempt to hide it. He didn't want to believe the slowly crystallizing suspicion. "Not yet," he said slowly. "But I'll find him. Indian Joe said some things. . . ."

He saw the involuntary stiffening of her back, but she didn't turn. "What did he say?"

Ben smiled a little. "Nothin' I can be sure of. He tried to hide what he knew, but a man who's not used to lyin' will always give himself away a little."

She wheeled to face him again. "I'll find out where Jet

is," she said. "I can find out for you!"

Ben frowned. "That mightn't be safe. Does anyone know you've talked to me?"

She shook her head emphatically. "I been careful."

"I'd ruther you didn't," Ben said. "If they thought you was goin' to tell me—"

"You needn't worry." She smiled thinly. "Men like to talk to me. I can learn without a man even knowin' he's told me what I wanted to know."

Did she mean that of him, too? Ben wondered. Or was he wronging her? Could any woman act so well, feigning love, calling up tears from a dry well?

"You just don't do anythin'—I mean, don't stir things up till I come back."

"I'll be goin' to Joe's funeral," Ben said.

She seemed thoughtful. "The men'll come back for a drink after that," she said. "Some won't go, but they'll be thinkin' about it. That'll make it easier to start talk goin'." She crossed over to Ben and stared up at his face, her eyes moving to take in every line and feature as if she wanted to print them on her mind. "Be careful, Ben Webber. I'll be back here soon as it's dark. Don't do nothin' till then. You promise?"

Ben nodded. "I'll be waitin'," he said.

Fifteen

It was late afternoon. A bell tolled, slow and mournful, in the little church on the town side of the hill. Mr. Templeton, head uncovered and bowed, stood beside the open grave. Looking past him, Ben could see a portion of yellow pine board. On the far side of the grave was a small cluster of townspeople, mostly men and a few womenfolk that Ben didn't know. Nancy Pardee was among them, and Jake Howell, glowering unhappily. Not many people to show for so many years of living, Ben thought. In a way, however, the people who had come—and those who didn't care enough—to watch Joe laid to rest didn't seem really pertinent to his life. That had really ended when his eyes had gone and the time of fighting was over for him. This death was something that didn't have anything to do with his life or what he had been, any more than the half-blind, drunken shell of man had much to do with the keen-eyed, hard-riding Indian fighter of past years.

When the bell stopped there was a moment of stillness in which the wind sighed gently in the cottonwood. Then Mr. Templeton spoke, his voice deep and slow and mournful like the bell. For a moment Ben stared in wonder at the scrawny preacher whose apple bobbed so ridiculously in his throat that you couldn't take your eyes off it. His speaking voice, so precise and careful, had given no warning of the richness of sound that now rolled from his tongue, sound that seemed too big for the slenderness of the man. Then Ben found himself listening to the majesty of an almost forgotten psalm. . . .

". . . the days of our years are threescore years and ten; and if by reason of strength they be fourscore years, yet is their strength labor and sorrow; for it is soon cut off, and we fly away. . . ."

And, listening, Ben gave his own meaning to the words, thinking that a man should not live beyond his time, for then he became less than he was. The preacher's voice rolled through the valley between the hills, and Ben was taken back in memory to long-forgotten nights when his father had read to the family in the Illinois farmhouse, his voice swelling warm and deep in the small room, his big-featured face magnificently impressive in the flickering light of the fire.

At last the service ended. There was a brief pause, followed by the utter finality of the first thud of earth thrown into the grave. Ben raised his eyes to Nancy Pardee and her glance met his. There was sadness and regret in her face, but as Ben started toward her she turned quickly and walked away. The group of people around the grave began to break up slowly. Ben stopped. What could he say to her? Nothing had changed.

Frowning, he stood near Joe's grave. How could he make the old man speak to him from the grave? Was there anything in his manner, his evasions, his choice of words that could speak for him now in Ben's memory? There had been conviction in his relating of the murder of Pardee. He had believed Jet guilty. The old man would have done a lot for free whisky, but he would not have borne false witness to murder. It must have been something else, something he could justify concealing, something he didn't consider important, a garnish of falsehood over the truth.

He hadn't known which grave was Jet's. Even with poor vision, even though he'd dug at night, it shouldn't have been so hard for him to point out which grave was new when he had dug them all. Unless—

Ben felt the chill of sudden thought, like an animal's quivering awareness of something strange and unexpected lying nearby in wait. If what he suspected of Jet's death was true, why should they have got the old man out at night to dig the grave? Why have a witness who might talk— unless he was already there?

As Joe had been there behind the stable.

Ben's eyes flicked alertly over the graveyard, noting the clear separation of two areas, the lower one where Joe now lay with the preacher's blessing, the upper rows set into the slope of the hill, devoid mostly of any stones or markings. He had presumed that Jet lay there. His feelings had blinded him as surely as clouded eyes had obscured Joe's vision.

Impulsively Ben started after the preacher, who had been the last of those around the grave to leave. Ben's long strides closed up the gap between him and the smaller man, who turned when he heard the steps behind him. The startled question in his face turned into displeasure.

"Mr. Templeton!" Ben called to stop him.

The preacher waited till Ben came up. He swallowed nervously. "Yes, Mr. Webber? I'm afraid I must be getting back—"

"I won't be keepin' you long," Ben said. "I was hopin' you might be able to help me some."

"If it's about your son . . ."

"It is," Ben admitted. "And I recall you sayin' you weren't present at his burial."

"That's quite true. It was done in haste that night, and in any event I couldn't have been part of the service."

"Your words just now sounded fine," Ben said. "They didn't seem to fit just a special kind of man."

"They are not my words," the preacher said stiffly, drawing himself up with great dignity. "But I must choose where they are appropriate."

"No offense, Mr. Templeton," Ben said. "Might be you could still help me. Maybe you don't know where my son was buried—but you just might be able to tell me where he wasn't."

The preacher looked taken aback. "I don't quite see . . ."

"You'd know for a fact if he was buried in the lower part," Ben said. "Now wouldn't you?"

"Yes," Mr. Templeton said slowly. "He wasn't, of course."

"There's only one grave that I can see in the upper part that's fresh enough," Ben said. "Would you be knowin' of anybody buried there this past week other than Jet Webber? Joe mentioned a stranger."

The preacher gasped. "But—but there must be more than one. You must be mistaken, Mr. Webber. There was a stranger killed in a gunfight last week."

"You're sure he was buried on the slope?"

Mr. Templeton stared at him. "Quite sure, Mr. Webber. I didn't perform a service—but I did have occasion to come to the graveyard that day. I couldn't help seeing the new grave."

Ben held still, letting the meaning of this fact expand in his mind. At length he nodded slowly. "I thank you, Mr. Templeton," he said.

The preacher looked bewildered. "But I'm afraid I don't understand."

"Nor I. But I reckon I'm beginning to," Ben said.

He said no more, and after a moment Mr. Templeton began to edge away from him, puzzled and unsure of himself, finally turning his back and marching off, his manner stiff and prim and a little too hasty. Ben waited until he had rounded the curve of the hill and was lost to sight. Then, with a purposeful stride, he swung back. He passed through the graveyard with hardly a glance at it.

His route brought him around to the far side of the hill into the deserted stretch behind the stable and its corral, an area sparsely wooded and overgrown with mesquite bush tall enough to conceal a man. It was a place where two men might meet to talk in secret, or a place where one might lie in wait to dry-gulch another. In the day kids might play here at hiding from each other, but they wouldn't pay any mind to a small patch of ground that had been overturned. There was little chance that curious folk would grub around hunting for a grave.

And not much chance they'd find it easy if they hunted.

Sixteen

Dusk came late to the angry arm of rock thrusting its red fist up at the sky, but it came early to the town which lay below in the shadow of the peak. From his window on the second floor of the hotel, Ben could see the broken plain to the east still golden in the sun long after his room turned cool and gray with shadows. He waited with impatience for the night to come. Stretched out on his back on the creaking bed, which was too short for him, and letting his feet dangle over the edge, Ben locked his hands behind his neck and willed the gnawing hunger for action to be still.

It was strange how easily a man could blind himself, Ben thought, how he could let the way he felt distort the very shape and color of things, make distances look wrong, hide truth and make the false seem true. A man's emotions were like a milky cloud in front of his eyes. If you were lucky, you did something that let the sun shine in on your mind through the mist and everything reverted to its normal size and meaning. It made you wonder how much you really knew about yourself, and it showed how little reason you had to judge another. How could you say a man acted thus and so for this reason or that, when you couldn't even say for sure about yourself?

A man could believe a great many foolish notions about himself. He could look kindly upon his image as a man of peace, pretending not to see the savage that was only covered over with fine clothes and soft words. He could tell himself that his sight was clear and true when he couldn't see the shape of things beyond his nose. He could find without much searching righteous words to justify his anger or loving words to make his lust look decent. He could even believe his life was over and done when it wasn't. . . .

It was fully dark when Julie Larkin came. The light rapping on the door brought Ben swinging off the bed to his feet, instantly alert, his hand reaching to scoop the Winchester from the floor beside the bed, his movements controlled and quick and quiet. Gun ready, he waited, motionless.

"Ben? It's Julie. Open the door."

He set down the gun and let her in. She stepped in quickly and shut the door, leaning against it. Her breath came short and fast as if she had been running or excited. In the darkness Ben could see the whites of her eyes.

"I'll put on a light," he said.

"No!" She touched his arm lightly. "It's best not to. If anybody seen me through the window . . ."

She let the hint of danger go unsaid, giving it magnitude. She moved close to him and her hands found his chest. Their touch burned through his shirt.

"If you still mean to go through with it," she said, keeping her voice low and secretive, "I've found out what you wanted."

"You know I mean to."

"Yes. I reckon you have to." The words came out reluctant and resigned. "I wish it weren't so, Ben honey."

"How'd you find out?"

"I—I have ways. The boys all know me and they trust me." She paused. "They think I'm Matson's girl."

"Uh-huh."

"Ben! *You* don't think that!"

"I've no reason to."

"I have to do what he tells me," she said. "I work for him. But that's all, Ben honey. That's all!"

Ben was silent. He was glad of the darkness. Even so he was too much aware of her—the soft caress of her fingers, the flower smell, the warmth of flesh so close to him, a body that would be as soft and warm and quivering beneath his hands as a frightened dove. Even in the darkness his mind brought back the picture of her mouth, swelling ripe and red, and of her bare shoulders with their satin sheen. But it wasn't quite so mind-confusing as the sight of her. Now he could listen to her voice and hear it clearly. In darkness you could taste the flavor of a spoken word without so much distraction. If a woman called you "honey" in the dark, you could tell if she meant it.

"Did you learn who buried Jet?" Ben asked.

She hesitated. "Red Morrell and Chico. I reckon that's why they were the ones picked to jump you, because they were already in on what had happened."

Ben nodded to himself. That much seemed true enough. "They told you where they put him?"

"No, not them. I didn't dare ask them." She gave a shiver. "That Chico, you never know what he's thinkin'. And Red's almost as bad. But Red talks sometimes. He told one of the other men about Jet. Seems they found him hangin', but he was already dead. The posse was gone. Red come back into town and told Matson. He had them get a coffin and give Jet a decent buryin'. Leastwise, that's what I was told."

Without mirth, Ben smiled a little to himself in the darkness. It was funny how, when he couldn't see her, he could sense it when she picked her words carefully.

"If that's all it was," he said slowly, "why would Matson try to hide it from me?"

"I—I don't know. Maybe he just wants things left alone. I reckon he would if—if he give Jet orders to shoot Pardee!"

It didn't hold water, Ben thought, but maybe they thought it didn't have to. They figured they were dealing with a man who was easily fooled. He'd given them reason enough to think so.

"Ben, why is it so important to you to find him? Why does it matter so?" She moved against him. Her face was tilted up, a dim pale oval, and he didn't have to see it to know the anxiety that was in her eyes. "I'm scared, honey! I'm scared somethin' will happen to you!"

Gently Ben held her away from him. "Nothin' is gonna happen," he said. "And I can't explain why I have to find Jet. You just tell me where to go."

"I—I'll have to show you. No use my tryin' to tell you where it is. I'll have to take you to it."

Ben hesitated. "I reckon you would," he said. "At night I wouldn't find it alone, not with Red Peak havin' such a crowded graveyard."

He could feel the relaxation of tension in her, the unconscious reflex of relief. It saddened him. If he'd needed more proof he had it now. Reluctantly he let his hands drop away from her arms.

"That's right enough," Julie was saying. "I'll know which one it is myself from what I was told, but it'd be hard explainin' to someone else, especially someone not knowin' the graveyard well."

Ben reached for the Winchester. "We'd best be leavin' then," he said. "It's dark enough now so's we won't be seen."

"No!" Her protest was urgent. "It's too early! There's lots of Matson's men still in the street and others might be ridin' in from the north. The trail goes close there to the graveyard, too close. We might be seen or heard. Besides, I'd be missed at the saloon. I'll have to get back there now."

Ben felt a knot of tension twisting slowly across his belly. So that was it. She was supposed to make him wait. It was easy now to see how Matson had used her all the while, first to find out what his purpose was in coming to Red Peak, then to get close to him so that he'd talk to her, reveal anything he had learned or share his secret suspicions. And now to keep him pinned down in the hotel.

Aloud he said, "It's a chance I'll have to take. You won't have to stay with me—just show me where it is."

"No, Ben!" She moved up close to him again. She had a way of edging closer to a man when she wanted you to give special heed to her words, as if her body might plead better than her voice. The thought was an ugly one and Ben felt ashamed of it.

"Listen to me," Julie urged, leaning so her softness pressed against the lean hard length of him. "I can get away later. I—I can pretend to go upstairs. That's what I'm supposed to do anyways, so I won't be missed then." Her voice seemed to blush for her, and Ben wondered if she was as clever with her flesh, if she could tell her cheeks to grow pink at will. "I'll sneak out and you can meet me. It'll be safer then. Folks in town that want to sleep will be sleepin', and the others will all be in the Nugget full of drink. Another hour or two won't matter, honey, and it'll be safer then."

Ben waited, seeming to consider what she said. "I reckon that makes sense," he said slowly.

"Sure it does. You'll see, Ben honey. I'll meet you—let's see—under the big cottonwood behind the hill. You know the one?"

"Yep. What time?"

"At—at nine o'clock. I reckon I can get away by then or close to it without anybody noticin'. Promise me you'll wait till then?"

In spite of himself, in spite of knowing how she'd tried to use him and how close she'd come to succeeding, Ben hesitated. Lies came hard to him.

"Ben! Promise me, honey!" Her body strained urgently

against him. "Promise you'll wait!"

"I'll be there at nine," he said.

She took it as agreement. For a moment longer she clung to him. "And Ben, even if you should change your mind—"

"I won't."

"But even if you should—if you thought to let Jet stay where he is and forget this need to take him back, I'll still be there. You hear me, honey? I'll come to you."

Ben had to steel his voice, trying to keep the harshness out of it. "I heard."

Her lips reached in the darkness for his mouth. They promised more than any words. With the lingering hesitation of reluctance she drew away. Ben made no move. Her dress rustled as she slipped over to the door.

"At nine," she whispered.

When the door opened he saw her for a second outlined in the light from the corridor. Her mouth still pouted from the moment's kiss and her eyes held yearning. He'd forgotten how a woman learned to use her eyes.

Then she was gone, and he couldn't hide or deny to himself the sinking emptiness of regret. Fleetingly he wondered once more if he would have seen her so clearly in the darkness if he had not so recently been reminded of a different kind of woman. She played on a man's pride, and there was nothing more likely to make a man betray himself.

Ben shook his body like a horse rising from a roll in the dirt. The gesture goaded him into action. He grabbed for his hat and his rifle.

Seventeen

In the corridor he hesitated. They might be watching the hotel to make sure he waited. Most likely they'd post a man across the street out front, not figuring he had reason to suspect the girl. Ben turned away from the stairs and followed the hallway toward the rear of the hotel. It ended where a window faced the back. Ben extinguished the wall lamp, throwing the hall into darkness. Flattening against the wall he peered out. Just below the window was the new roof of the extension Luke Harris was building. That made an exit easy. He could crawl out to the edge and drop off by the side where it was darkest. Even if a man was watching the rear door there was a good chance Ben wouldn't be seen.

The window wasn't locked and it slid up easily and quietly. If Luke Harris had made it he was a good carpenter, Ben thought as he hooked a leg over the ledge. Red Peak had reason to be—

He froze. Instinct made him deny his body's clamor for sudden withdrawal. He held himself absolutely still, awkwardly perched half in and half out of the window. His eyes studied the dark bulk of the cliff that rose steeply behind the hotel and the town. He wasn't sure what had brought him the chill of warning—the mere remembering how the cliff rose commandingly above him or the faint spark of brightness he'd caught on the fringe of his vision. The light might have been reflection. Even without it he had to take the wall of rock into account. It wasn't so sheer or unbroken that a man couldn't climb it and find ledges to hide on, looking down from a safe niche at the hotel.

It came again—a flaring redness above and to the right of the hotel from a point halfway up the cliff's face. It wasn't the sudden explosion of a match. The dim light glowed and faded quickly. It was the kind of brightness a cigarette might make when puffed in the darkness with a man's hand cupped over the red ash.

A sentry should be more careful, Ben thought. A man could die from making a mistake like that. And another man might live because of it.

Without reasoning it out he knew the man was not posted on the cliff to give him further warning. That stage was past. Matson was in the open now, ready to take his chances on accounting for Ben's death. Matson wanted to keep him trapped in the hotel for a time—and Ben thought he knew why.

With painful slowness he drew back his leg. In darkness the eye will pick out sudden movement where a motionless or creeping shadow will go unseen. He didn't begrudge the extra seconds it took or the sweat it brought to his forehead where his hatband fitted snugly. When he was back in the hall he took another minute to ease the window closed. During this time his mind roved quickly over a series of moves, weighing and discarding them. When he finally turned back along the hall he knew his only possible exit was right where he could be seen best.

He walked out the front door of the hotel. Stepping down into the street he felt as naked as he had that time he'd led an unarmed peace mission into the Sioux camp, three men facing an army of war-minded Indians. But he'd been safer then. He'd trust an Indian to honor a white flag before he'd gamble on one of Matson's men taking a shot at him from cover.

The street was busy at this early hour of the night. Ben had to skip out of the way of a wagon rolling into town from the south. There were horses tethered along the rail bordering the walk. Cigars and cigarettes sparked and glowed where men stood talking, and there were lights in many of the buildings throwing their feeble yellow gleam into the shadows of the street.

Ben walked easily, not hurrying, the Winchester drooping from the crook of his elbow. He saw no point in trying to pick out which of the obscure figures along the boardwalk might be watching him. There would be one or more, and they'd follow him. Better to risk a bullet here in the open street than in a quiet back alley.

He turned into the restaurant and walked down the line to a stool at the end of the counter. He ordered meat and potatoes and cooked cabbage. While he waited he watched the door. The first man who entered after him looked too soft and fat to be dangerous, and the second wore a working waddie's faded jeans and a cumbersome jacket. It was the third newcomer who had the lean, hawk-eyed toughness that Ben had been expecting. His gun looked big on his narrow hip, and the holster was tilted back so far that when he sat you'd have thought the gun would slip out on its own. He took a seat midway along the counter.

Ben wolfed down his food. He wasn't hungry and his belly wasn't easy. The food all clogged together and made an uneasy weight down there in the pit. But a man was supposed to come into a restaurant to eat.

With a sigh he pushed his empty plate away and stirred sugar into a fresh cup of coffee. The man behind the counter came to remove Ben's plate.

"Got a bank out back," Ben asked, raising his voice a little, "where a man might make a deposit?"

The counterman grinned. "Yep." He jerked his thumb toward the rear of the restaurant. "Door right there around the corner. You'll see it."

Ben thanked him. He'd already set a silver dollar down on the counter. "I'll be having more hot coffee when I get back."

He rose casually and went out the back door. It was necessary to take the Winchester and he knew that if he hadn't already given his game away taking the gun would do it, but he had no choice. Once outside he saw the narrow, sentinel shape of the privy set well away from the main row of buildings. Instead of walking toward it he stepped quickly into the deep shadow flanking the doorway.

There wasn't long to wait. The lean gunman appeared in the door, the light from behind throwing his shadow out before him. His hand was on the butt of his gun. Ben held his breath and let the man step out. He was peering toward the privy and didn't even see the heavy stock of the rifle slashing down to club him behind the ear. It knocked him right off his feet. He grunted and sprawled full length on the ground. The reflex action of his gun hand brought his revolver clear of the holster as he fell, but there wasn't the strength in his nerveless fingers to squeeze the trigger.

Ben glanced through the door. The angle of the narrow corridor cut him off from a view of the counter. No sound indicated that he had been seen. He bent and lifted the sagging weight of the gunman, hauling him erect. Then he stooped and let the unconscious man drape over his shoulder like a sack. He carried the limp figure out behind the privy where the ground dropped away into a shallow gully. Dumping him on his face, Ben folded the man's arms behind his back and tied them with the bandanna from his neck. Then he used the gunman's belt to hobble his feet.

That done, he stood for a moment looking down. He was breathing deeply from exertion. He knelt and examined the body. A lump had already started to rise behind the gunman's ear but his heart was beating evenly. Ben felt neither satisfaction nor anger. The man meant nothing to him—but at least it would be some time before he could sound any alarm to Matson.

For another minute Ben watched the rear door of the restaurant. No one appeared. Then Ben set off along the gully, keeping low, heading toward the north end of town. He felt the need for haste now—he'd lost too much time—but he controlled the impulse to run. A man running on unfamiliar, broken ground not only made too much noise, but he was also too busy keeping his feet to watch what lay ahead of him. Or behind.

The gully petered out short of the final group of buildings which marked the end of the street. Here Ben paused. He weighed the chance of crossing the street without being seen and then using the stable as cover till he got behind it. In the end he chose to follow the route he'd used that afternoon. He swung wide to the right, circling around the small church and its garden and continuing a hundred yards north before he cut back behind the graveyard. Just as he had reasoned, nothing disturbed its solemn stillness. He kept angling toward the right, detouring to get extra cover. When he was sure he had gone far enough he turned back toward town. A low hill blocked his way. Using what concealment the mesquite bushes and trees offered he worked his way up the slope and down the town side of the hill. Coming downslope into the deserted area behind the stable he crept more cautiously, listening for the faintest warning sound ahead.

It came so suddenly, so close to him, that his nerves vibrated like plucked strings.

"Dammit, Chico, you sure this is the place?"

"Si, I am sure."

Ben sank to the ground. He flattened himself under a clump of mesquite, mindless of the tough bare branches that raked and scratched his face. For a moment he lay motionless, his scalp still tingling at the narrow margin by which he'd escaped blundering right into them in the darkness. Now his straining ears picked out small, significant sounds and he wondered how he had missed them. Chunk. Thud. Chunk. Thud. A grunt and a low curse. The steady dig and lift and throw, dual rhythms run too close together for one shovel. Both men were digging.

He began to inch forward, wriggling in the coarse grass like a long snake, guided by the sounds, still unable to see the two men or place them exactly.

"Damn! I coulda swore we never dug so deep."

"I hit it, I theenk."

He placed them now, scarcely three rods away from him. And he heard quite clearly the clunk of heavy metal striking wood. The sound did something to Ben. A kind of haze formed in his brain and laid a thin red web before his eyes. He came to his knees, forgetting the need for caution. A rage as hot as lust shot through him. He started forward heedlessly. A branch bent and snapped under his foot.

"What's that?"

"Huh?"

"You hear something?"

"You are jumpy, amigo. What is there to hear?"

Ben crouched on the ground. His body shook with the struggle for control. The blood drummed in his veins and a muscle spasm jerked his cheek. No! he breathed. Not this way. Not this animal lust to kill. No. Take it slow. Easy. The boy is dead. Nothing can hurt him now. What will it gain to charge in like a maddened stallion? Do you want to make it easy for them to cut you down?

"I tell you I heard somethin'. Maybe that guy got out of the hotel."

"He wouldn't know of this place, I theenk."

"Yeah? Well, I'm gonna make sure."

There was silence then, followed by the stealthy rustle of movement to Ben's left but approaching his position. The knowledge of new danger cleared the last of the haze from his mind. Immobile, he waited with his rifle poised and ready as Red Morrell worked closer. He wondered what Chico was doing. The sounds of digging had stopped. Morrell moved clumsily in the darkness and Ben was able to follow his slow progress easily. The line of Morrell's path would bring him within ten feet of the spot where Ben crouched.

Morrell's dark bulk was suddenly visible through the tangled nest of branches separating them. He had stopped, listening. Ben held his breath. There was no way of knowing whether the thin mesquite screen would hide his long shadow close to the ground. If the gunman took another step and looked directly at him he wouldn't be able to wait for a reaction. He would have to—

"Sssst!"

"What—!"

Morrell whirled. Ben saw his arm move, glimpsed the dull gleam of metal.

"No, amigo!" Chico's voice cracked like a whip.

"You! Goddammit, Chico, I almost killed you!"

Chico snickered. "I do not theenk so."

Morrell cursed. "Whatta ya mean, sneakin' up on me like that? You crazy?"

"You heard something. If it was true, I would not want you to have the fun all by yourself."

"Yeah? Well, I reckon I was hearin' things. There's nobody here."

"If there was, amigo, you scared him off with all the noise you made, eh?"

Chico giggled again. The high-pitched laughter shivered along Ben's spine and he felt his skin contract with sudden chill. Chico had stolen as near to him as Morrell. And Ben hadn't even heard him.

The two men crashed away through the brush, no longer bothering to be quiet. Ben crept along behind them, letting their noisy progress cover his own. When they broke into a clearing and stopped suddenly he lay still, waiting. After a moment the digging began again. He edged closer. Shovels scraped against wood. Once. Twice. Clearing dirt from the top of the coffin, cutting the earth away at the sides. The red haze filmed his eyes again. Jet's coffin.

He reached the fringe of a small clearing. In the center of it, standing waist-deep in a roughhewn grave, Red and

148

Chico worked without speaking, grunting with effort. Ben's eyes picked out the shapes of two gun belts on the ground. The weight of a gun was awkward on your hip when you tried to handle a shovel. Chico's gun was several steps away from the grave, but Morrell's was within his reach. Ben reined his anger tight and hard, forcing himself to wait.

Chico paused, panting, and leaned on his shovel. "I theenk we might pry off the top now."

"Whatta ya mean?" Morrell grunted. "Your end ain't clear. And this end has gotta be wider."

Chico shrugged and went back to work. Ben waited until Morrell had also stooped to dig, both hands on his shovel. Then he stepped out fast.

"Hold it right there," he called harshly.

Two heads jerked toward him. As he came erect Morrell's mouth gaped open. His eyes flicked toward his gun belt.

"If you want to die right now," Ben said, "you can try for your guns."

Morrell began to curse savagely. "I told you I heard him!" he raged.

"I am not so smart, I theenk," Chico murmured. His white teeth gleamed in the darkness.

Ben stalked closer, reserving only a corner of his gaze for Chico, centering his stare on Morrell and his gun. He could almost read the uneasy balance of Morrell's thoughts, the rapid weighing of his chances.

"I know what you're thinkin'," Ben said softly. "But you won't make it." He halted two paces from the lip of the grave, letting the Winchester's barrel dip toward Morrell's chest. "I'd get one of you first. I reckon you'd have to guess which one."

Morrell let loose a string of epithets. "I shoulda put a bullet through you last night," he snarled. "Well, you're gonna have to shoot quick and straight to pull this off, cowboy, and I don't think you got the guts!"

"Do not be so hasty, amigo," Chico said, still grinning, still holding a shovelful of earth half raised at the point where Ben's command had stopped him. "I do not theenk I am ready to die just yet."

Ben smiled thinly, grimly. He'd almost hoped that one of them would make a move. He reached out with his toe and caught the loop of Morrell's gun belt, jerking it toward him. His eyes hard and wary, he stooped and slipped the gun from its holster, flinging it far out into the brush.

Slowly he eased erect. "Keep diggin'," he said. "You're gonna finish what you started. And then we're all goin' in to see the sheriff and have a talk."

Morrell spat. "If you think I'm gonna dig for you, cowboy, you're even stupider than I figured."

Chico's soft voice broke in. "Sure, we deeg," he said. "Why not?"

He bent and straightened up fast. His hands flicked in a blur of motion and a shovel load of dirt flew toward Ben's face. There was no time to duck. Moist clods of earth smacked his face, blinding him, and the years of peace, of conditioning against violence, betrayed him now, delaying the fractional pressure of his finger that would have sent a bullet tearing into Morrell's thick chest. Ben stumbled backward, pawing damp soil away from his eyes. His heels caught and he fell.

He lit hard on his shoulder blades. As he twisted around to face the grave Morrell was clambering over the edge. Ben caught the flash of Chico's arm raising and saw the glitter of a knife blade as he set himself to throw. Ben fired from the ground, levered and fired again. The first shot hit the Mexican's shoulder and threw him back. The second turned his white grin into the gaping red maw of death.

Ben pivoted too late. Morrell's boot caught him on the side of his face. The rifle flew out of his hands. Stars burst inside his head, and his ear felt as if it had been torn off. Instinctively he rolled away. The next kick missed him, throwing Morrell off balance. Ben caught the swinging foot, twisted and heaved, taking Morrell off his feet.

Ben staggered up. Morrell was scrambling off his knees as Ben's eyes tried to focus on him. He charged in and Ben swung, hitting pole-hard flesh. Morrell's big fist seemed to capsize his chest. He felt the air rush out of his lungs. Weakly Ben struck and hit again. The blows bounced off Morrell's body like a hoe off solid rock. Ben gave ground, blinking to clear his vision, sucking air back into his chest. He had the odd feeling that all this had happened before. And it had, only this time he wasn't drunk. There was still a ringing in his torn right ear, but he could feel strength surging back into his arms. Morrell had almost succeeded in finishing him with that first kick.

The gunman's eyes glittered with killing fever as he crowded after Ben, and it came to Ben that Morrell wouldn't settle for anything short of his death now. Hate boiled up in him, hate for the killers, for the despoilers of Jet's grave, for the soilers of his name.

He dug in his heels and waited. Morrell rushed in fast,

but he telegraphed his roundhouse swing. Ben stepped inside it and drove his fists in two short, vicious, chopping blows that smashed Morrell's nose and spread blood over his suddenly distorted face. Morrell grunted and stopped dead. Ben hit him with another piston stroke as hard as he could and stepped back to let him fall.

The gunman swayed, blinked, shook his head and lumbered forward once more. Ben met his charge, taking heavy blows on arms and shoulders. He felt weariness already weighting his arms and legs. For the first time he glimpsed defeat. Morrell was bigger, harder, younger, stronger. Ben dropped his shoulder and drove it into Morrell's heavy belly like a battering ram. Grunting, Morrell backed up. Then his thick arms caught Ben and wrapped around him, squeezing, fists locking at the base of Ben's spine. He felt himself being lifted off his feet. His back bent under the painfully tightening pressure. Ben shoved the heel of his palm under Morrell's jaw and rammed his head back hard. The pressure of his arms only increased. The pain was making Ben dizzy, and he knew that there was no more give left in his spine, that it was stretched taut like a supple green stick that will bend only so far before it snaps. He got both arms free and smashed two quick, brutal blows with the flat edge of his hand against Morrell's neck, behind and under his ear. The pressure slackened fleetingly. In that second Ben braced and tore free of the hug. His foot hooked behind Morrell's ankle and he shoved hard. The big man toppled like a felled tree.

Ben waited for him. Morrell rolled away from the expected boot. When he faced Ben, crouching, there was something new in his face—fear. His eyes flicked to the side. Ben saw it but understood too late. As he leaped forward Morrell's hand wrapped around the handle of the shovel. He swung at Ben's diving body. The flat of the blade cracked against Ben's shins and knocked him sprawling.

He looked up to see the shovel high over his head, slashing down in a vicious, sharp-edged plunge. He threw himself to the side. The edge of the blade dug into the ground inches from his head, driving so deep that it stuck. As Morrell tried to jerk it free Ben grabbed the handle and drove to his feet. Deliberately he smashed his fist directly into Morrell's throat.

The gunman gurgled with pain and staggered back, clawing at his throat. Ben followed him, driving short, chopping blows into the pulpy face. With a choked curse Morrell plunged in close, grabbing Ben's arms. His knee slashed up. Ben twisted, taking bruising punishment on his hip but avoiding the crippling kick in his groin. An elbow caught his mouth. He tried to break free and failed to see Morrell's bullet head dip down and lash suddenly upward. It cracked like a chunk of granite against Ben's jaw.

The ground reeled wildly and there was a roaring in his head. For a moment he felt consciousness flickering. Out of the void he glimpsed the wavering image of a woman's face, dark with sorrow. Her lips moved and he listened for Ellen's voice, but, mysteriously, it wasn't her voice that reached through the curtain of semi-consciousness to speak to him but that of another woman, a woman with brown hair heavy against her neck and hazel eyes as soft and soothing as her words.

"Be quiet now. You're hurt. Be quiet."

"I had to come back," he mumbled. "A man sees somethin' in a woman that he needs. You hear me, Nancy?"

"Don't talk, Ben. Don't say it."

"I had to come. You got to understand. Jet didn't do it. He
didn't kill your brother. . . ."

Ben fought back to clarity, and now it was the red blob of
Morrell's face that weaved before him, eyes glittering with
triumph as he moved in. Ben swung with all the work-
hardened strength that was left in his arm and shoulder. The
shock of the blow jolted all the way back into his chest.
Something gave in his left fist and his arm tingled.

And Morrell was down. Ben stood over him, his tall
body swaying. "Get up," he said hoarsely.

Morrell crawled to his hands and knees. Ben took his
time and kicked him in the head. Morrell went down again
on his face. Ben watched him, his left arm hanging limp
and useless at his side. He knew if Morrell got up again
Ben Webber would be finished.

"Get up," he said.

But it was all over.

Eighteen

He had trouble standing straight and when he moved his
ankles rocked as if they were too weak to support him. He
stepped over Morrell's unconscious figure and staggered
across to the grave. Chico lay crumpled in a corner, his
black eyes open and staring, his mouth and part of his jaw
blown away in such a manner that he still seemed to wear
an evil grin.

Ben sat down heavily. He had no sense of time and he

didn't know whether he rested there at the edge of the grave for one minute or ten. The brutal beating he'd taken had left him numb in his feelings as well as in his body. He thought of the hate and anger that had triggered his fists, and for the second time that day he saw himself in sharper perspective, seeing that this rage had been only distant kin to the wild joy of battle he had known in his youth. That taint of violence which he had denied in himself and feared in Jet for so long was muted, changed by the years of peace and love he had known. Even the drunken brawl he'd started the night before had been something different, the explosion of bottled-up anguish—a more civilized devil than the one he once had battled. Looking inside himself, Ben Webber knew that he was really his own man at last, more truly because he understood himself. There was anger in him, and a capacity for hate, and the willingness to kill if need be to save his life or revenge another, but these were part of a man and the way he lived in his time.

If Ben had known himself sooner, Jet Webber might have lived and grown to be another kind of man. Ben thought in simple terms of the irony that a man always discovers himself too late.

After a time he found that he was staring at the fresh yellow of pine boards beneath his feet, half covered with damp earth. His mind revolved around the fact for several seconds before it crystallized into a need for action. Stiffly he dropped down into the grave. Because he could use only his right arm, it was an awkward business to pick up the limp body of Chico with its grotesquely grinning face and dump it over the edge. Ben rested then a minute before he groped for a shovel. Ignoring the pain in his hand and chest and head, he began methodically to scrape dirt from the top of the crude coffin.

In a short time the surface was clear. Realizing that he couldn't hope to raise the coffin alone now, he chopped away at the sides of the grave, working below the coffin's top, clearing a space that would allow him room for leverage. When he could get the blade of the shovel under the edge of the first board, he pried upward. Nails shrieked, resisted, and gave way. He loosened a second plank and tore it off.

Kneeling, he peered into the dark interior. He fumbled for a match and flicked it with his thumb. In the sudden yellow flare of light Jet Webber's face showed pale and shrunken, its good bones strongly outlined under the parchment skin. From the sockets of his eyes a busy, heedless horde of life crawled over his cheek and flowed down his smooth, unmarked neck above the black shirt. Sickness tugged at Ben's belly and he turned his head away. This was his son, but there was an endless chasm between this lifeless figure and the boy he'd loved and sent away. The memory of Jet's vital strength and pride and pent-up force flooded his mind and brought the sting of tears to his eyes.

He blinked and forced himself to light another match and look again inside the coffin. The meaning of that smooth, pale neck, unmarked by any rope, slashed through his grief. In the same moment his eyes picked out the crease of a bullet along Jet's skull, beginning behind his ear.

After a while he stood, head bowed. His brain moved sluggishly, slow to follow the trail of the stunning knowledge he'd discovered, a fact suspected without reason or explanation, now confirmed.

He heard the unmistakable click of a gun being cocked. There was an immediate stillness inside him. His head came up slowly and he saw the legs of horses. Saddle leather creaked as men shifted weight. Hooves crunched in the brush. A group of riders were spread around the clearing in a circle. A rifle and several drawn revolvers gleamed cold and gray.

"Hold your triggers!" someone said clearly.

One rider pushed out from the others, who looked on in silence as Ben stared at Nancy Pardee.

"I reckon we got here too late," she said.

"No," Ben said slowly. "I'd say you picked a good time."

As she swung down from the horse Ben clambered out of the grave. Her eyes took in Morrell's sprawled body and the shapeless huddle that had been Chico. A man swung down and turned Morrell over on his back. There was awe in his gaze as he looked up at Ben.

"He's alive," Ben said. And to Nancy Pardee he added, "I reckon he can tell you who shot your brother. I'd guess it was him or Chico."

She seemed too stunned to answer.

"Don't know as you should look, but you ought to know," Ben said. "My boy wasn't hanged. He was shot— from behind, I judge."

"But—the posse—"

"There weren't no posse," Ben said sharply. "And there wasn't any shootin' between Jet and Ross Pardee. I can't prove that yet, but I will."

She shook her head, bewildered. Her lips tightened with determination and she strode over to the edge of the grave, hesitated and slid down. Ben watched her. Many of the riders had dismounted, and they crowded close. Suddenly Nancy Pardee turned and leaned against the side of the grave. Her face was white and she was shaking. Ben knelt close to her.

"Oh, Ben!" she whispered.

"I figure your brother and my son were both killed," Ben said quietly. "Then they cooked up this story of the Pardee shootin', and they had to invent a hangin' to explain Jet's death. How they dragged Indian Joe into it I don't know. He knew part of the truth and that's why he was killed, but I don't think he knew all of it. That's the way I see it."

She looked up at him. The compassion in her eyes changed to sharp concern as she stared more closely at his face.

"You're hurt!" she cried.

Ben tried to smile through puffed lips. Conscious of the throbbing in his hand, he tried to keep it out of sight. "I've been clawed worse by a bear," he said.

"Help me out," she said abruptly.

Ben gave her his good hand and pulled her up. She turned toward the men watching them.

"Some of you don't know Ben Webber," she said, speaking up clearly. "Jet was his son, the man we thought killed Ross. From the look of things we were wrong. I reckon some of you should see for yourselves he wasn't hanged." She swung back to Ben. "These are some of the ranchers Ross tried to organize against Matson. This here's Zeke Lucas. We were havin' a meetin' in town and Zeke rode in late. When he stopped at the stable the boy workin' there now told him there was a fight goin' on back here— he'd heard shots. When Zeke told us about it, we figured we ought to investigate."

The man called Zeke lowered himself into the grave, peered wordlessly inside the coffin, turned back and crawled out. His mouth was a tight, flat line.

"He was shot, all right enough," Zeke Lucas said. "But that doesn't exactly prove he didn't shoot Ross."

"If part of the story was a lie," Nancy Pardee said angrily, "it stands to reason the whole thing was cooked up to fool us. Once we knew, or thought we knew, that Ross's killer was dead, we wouldn't be so hot to make more trouble. Matson fooled us! Now do some of you still feel it isn't time to take the law into our own hands?"

There was an angry muttering from the circle of men.

"All right, so maybe Webber didn't shoot Ross," one of them spoke up, an older cowboy with a worn, tired face. "That don't change things none. We knew all along that Matson was behind it one way or another. We still don't have a chance in the world trying to ride in and shoot it out with him and all those gunslicks!"

"I don't know what this is all about," Ben said. "But you won't have to go after Matson. I reckon that's my right."

They all stared at him in shocked surprise.

"Ben Webber, are you crazy?" Nancy Pardee cried. "You can't go after him alone!"

"I've got to."

"You wouldn't stand a chance," Zeke Lucas growled.

Ben shrugged. "It isn't somethin' I can argue," he said flatly. "If you want to back me, that's your doin'. But Matson's mine."

There was a moment's uneasy silence. Nancy Pardee stepped close to Ben and peered up at his face. "It won't help if you're killed too," she said gently. "Matson won't fight fair. Even if he did, you're no gunman and he is."

"So were his boys," Ben said.

For a moment longer Nancy studied him. "I reckon there's no stoppin' you," she said then. She wheeled to face the other men. "Well, are we goin' to let him go in there alone? Or are we goin' to back him?"

The men shifted uncertainly, looking at each other, each waiting for the next man to speak up.

Zeke Lucas took the lead. "How do you figure we can help?" he said to Ben.

Ben hesitated. It was true that this was their fight as well as his, though he would just as soon have acted on his own. "You can keep Matson's men off me," he said. "That's all I ask."

Zeke nodded. "We can be there, anyways," he said, raising his voice as he turned to the others. "We can give Ben Webber a fightin' chance against Matson. Any man that could take care of Chico and Red Morrell the way he did, maybe he can take Matson too. He's got the right to try!"

Another man nodded agreement. "I'll back him," he said. One by one, some reluctantly, some grimly, the others spoke. They wouldn't face a shooting match with Matson's hands in open battle, but they'd be there in the saloon when Ben walked in to challenge Matson.

"You git that far," one said, "an' there ain't nobody gonna shoot you in the back, by God!"

Ben nodded. He looked at Nancy Pardee with a mixture of gratitude and a deeper emotion he hadn't the nerve yet to name. "I've got somethin' else to do first," he said. "If your men will be in the Gold Nugget in about an hour, that's when I'll come."

"We'll be there," Nancy said.

Ben frowned. "Not you," he said. "I don't want no woman there. Especially you."

"Maybe I've got somethin' to say about that," she retorted.

"He's right, Miss Nancy," Zeke Lucas said. "Anyways, if you came in his place Matson would know somethin' was up."

Her lips tightened. "I'll not see you go against him while I stand by doin' nothin'!" she said firmly.

"You can help," Ben said. "You can see Morrell is taken care of—and Jet. And I may have another for you to talk to. I've a meetin' with Matson's girl."

Nancy looked surprised. A shadow of disappointment crossed her face. "*Matson's* girl?"

"You mean Julie?" one of the cowboys asked.

Ben nodded. "She tried to trick me. And maybe she fooled Jet, too. She claimed she was gonna marry him. I reckon she can tell me a few things I want to know."

He wondered if he was right in guessing that it was relief he saw now in Nancy's eyes.

"Tell us what you want," she said. "I'll see it's done."

Nineteen

He waited under the cottonwood. He heard her coming before he saw her. She was on foot and made her way slowly over the rough ground. As she came closer Ben could see how the blue satin dress she wore caught the dim light of a moonless night. Then he saw that a shawl covered the smooth white shoulders he couldn't put completely out of his mind. He stayed in shadow. Her head kept turning, eyes searching the darkness, but she didn't see him.

"Ben?" she called when she was close. "You there, Ben?"

He stepped clear of the tree. "Here, Julie."

"Oh!" She jumped back, startled. "I didn't see you."

"I been waitin' for you."

She came forward slowly. Ben saw the way her eyes kept looking behind him expectantly. "I—I didn't know if you'd be here."

"Why wouldn't I be?"

Her gaze peered narrowly at his face. "No reason, Ben, honey. Unless you'd changed your mind."

He felt no real anger toward her, even though she'd planned to lead him into an ambush, even though he was sure that she was partly guilty of Jet's death. It was hard not to see how pretty she was and to remember how she'd acted when she came to his room those first times. Even knowing that her kisses had been given by design didn't erase their imprint. He thought how easy it was for a woman like this one to lull a man's suspicions and make him forget what he knew of her—make him eager to forgive, if she'd just give him half a chance.

"You said you'd show me where the grave is," he said quietly.

"Sure. Sure I will, Ben. You brought a shovel?"

"I did."

After hesitating briefly she began to move away from him past the cottonwood, her glance roving as if she were measuring distances or seeking out landmarks. But her head kept coming up as she peered into the surrounding brush. Ben followed close after her.

"It's this way?" he asked.

"I—I think so. That's what I was told. It should be west of the tree."

"It's not."

She looked at him sharply. "What made you say that?"

"I know where it is, Julie."

Her eyes were puzzled now and she was frowning. Even in the dim light Ben could see the irritation and impatience beginning to rise in her. Her gaze slanted away from him to peck at the shadows behind.

"There's no one there to help you," he said.

Suspicion of the truth burst on her and she backed a step. "What do you mean, Ben? What are you tryin' to say?"

"I'm sayin' Red and Chico aren't comin', Julie."

She stiffened visibly. Her voice had lost some of its confidence. "Why would they be? I don't know what you—"

"Chico's dead," he interrupted coldly. "And Morrell won't be harmin' anybody for a spell. I didn't stay in the hotel, Julie, the way you wanted. I found Jet's body, so there's no use pretendin' any more about the grave. You knew he wasn't hanged, didn't you?"

"Not hanged! Ben, you're talkin' loco!"

"He was shot—just like I was supposed to be tonight."

"You can't think I had anythin' to do with it. We was gonna be married. You knew that!"

Ben stepped close to her and spoke roughly. "You told me. I reckon you told him the same, and I can see how he would have believed you. Was it easy to fool him, Julie?"

163

Her face changed suddenly. Scorn flashed in her eyes, and the mouth that had been so soft was like a knife's edge. "Yes!" she cried contemptuously. "Yes, it was easy! What do you think? He wasn't old like you. He was young! He wanted me! You think it wasn't easy to make him tell me what I wanted to know?"

"What did he tell you?" Ben asked softly.

She laughed. "Why not? You ain't gonna tell anybody. John Matson will kill you. You hear that, Ben Webber? He'll kill you! He's a real man!"

Pride throbbed fiercely in her ringing words, and in that instant Ben seemed to see her mind and heart naked before him. He felt a fleeting pity for her, for the woman's desperate love that could make her lie and cheat, so slavish that she'd crawl in the dirt to do a man's bidding. What kind of poverty of love in her life would make Matson's mean so much to her?

"Jet met Pardee that night," Julie said. "But he didn't kill him. He was gonna lend him money!" She laughed again. "He was runnin' out on Matson and throwin' in with Pardee and the ranchers." Contempt filled her voice. "He told me all about it, his lovin' Julie. Said he'd had enough of killin' and fightin'. That was your son, Ben Webber! He was yellow, you hear? He was runnin' out!"

Her final taunt didn't touch him. There was too much emotion swelling in his chest. This was his son—not a hardened killer but a man grown to maturity. Sadness deepened in him, but there was pride as well, the pride he'd known so many years before when the boy was young, a pride he'd thought never to know again.

"We see things different," Ben said. "But I'm grateful

to you."

"Grateful!"

"Yes. For reasons maybe you wouldn't understand."

His reaction confused and angered her. "I understand, all right enough. Don't think I don't understand."

Ben shifted tactics suddenly. His words lashed out accusingly. "You told Matson about Jet and Pardee. You knew where they were meetin' and you let them walk into an ambush. You as good as killed them yourself!"

"What of it?" she retorted sullenly. "They had it comin'."

"What about Indian Joe? Was he in on it, too?" Ben didn't give her time to think. "Was he part of it?"

"He didn't know nothin'. He was too blind—"

"But he's dead now, Julie! Would you say he had that comin'?"

Her face flushed. "I talk too much," she snapped. "But you won't be tellin'!"

Her hand was under her shawl. Ben saw it move and he struck instinctively, his hand snaking out to seize her wrist just as the blunt nose of a derringer broke into the open. Ben twisted hard as the gun barked and a bullet sang past his ear. The derringer dropped from her fingers and kicked up dust at her feet. She cried out and tried to free her arm, kicking at Ben's ankles as she fought him.

Then other figures were running toward them. Ben held Julie easily, releasing her when the others had surrounded them. She stumbled back and Nancy Pardee caught her none too gently.

"You hold her, Zeke," she said, shoving Julie into the hands of the man nearest her.

Zeke Lucas looked uncomfortable, but he held Julie's

struggling figure in his big hands.

"We heard some of it," Nancy said. "Enough to know you were right. I reckon we all owe you an apology—you and Jet. Most of all, I do."

"We were all fooled," Ben said. "If there's any owin', it's what's comin' to Matson."

Julie Larkin laughed harshly. Anger sparked in Nancy's eyes and she whirled on Julie. "Hold your tongue!" she snapped. "The men might treat you easy because you're a woman. That won't hold me back!"

Julie's lip curled in defiance but she checked the retort that started in her throat. Nancy glared at her for a moment before swinging stiffly back to Ben. Their eyes locked. Gradually the tension went out of her, the anger giving way, and her gaze softened.

"I'm glad it wasn't Jet killed Ross," she said.

"So am I."

Her lip quivered and she bit it. "Take care, Ben."

"Maybe I've reason to," he said. "Now."

Twenty

He skirted the town and came in from the south end, keeping to the deep shadows as much as he could. He had to chance the sentry still being on duty behind the hotel, but he doubted that the watch would have been kept this long. He slipped into the hotel the back way. The lobby was quiet, the woman dozing behind the counter. Ben got up to his room without meeting anyone.

The gun belt was on the table where he'd left it. Zeke Lucas had offered him a gun and had looked dubious and worried when Ben rejected it. Ben hadn't tried to explain. Even for himself he hadn't found the words. He had simply known that it was right for him to come for Jet's gun.

Through the window he studied the street below. It was strangely quiet. Horses stood patiently along the rails at the sides, and here and there men still smoked silently along the boardwalk, but the street itself was dark and empty. There was suspense in the stillness, as if the town was waiting for what this night would bring. Nancy Pardee's ranchers would be in the Gold Nugget, standing at the bar, around the faro tables, or by the piano, nervously watching for Ben's appearance. He didn't know how much he could count on them when the showdown came. His gaze flicked across to the sheriff's office. He had a hunch Jake Howell might be hard to find when the shooting started. The sheriff seemed to have a nose for trouble, and trouble hung ominous in the air, as strong as the scent of pine in high mountains.

The words Nancy Pardee had once spoken of Jet in anger came back to him again. "Your Jet was only a gun! A gun doesn't need a reason to go off. All you do is pull the trigger!"

Only a gun. Jet had proved himself much more than that—how much Ben would never know. Maybe a man never really knew his son, Ben less than most. He remembered some of the stories he'd heard during the past five years. They may have had a part of truth in them, and the boy had surely done some things he was accountable for to his Maker. But he was one of a wild breed, born to a time of quick passions and sudden violence. He was a kind you wouldn't be seeing so much more in the years to come, and the world then might be an easier place to be born in and to grow to be a man and find your place and your woman and your piece of land. Then men like Ben himself wouldn't turn to violence as the only answer. Jet had been a gunfighter, and you couldn't explain away all of what he was or what he'd done. But in the end he had weighed the right and wrong of Matson's fight with the ranchers and he'd sided with the right. That was enough for Ben. It was more than he had ever hoped for.

The ranchers had helped Ben raise the coffin and seal it closed again. They'd found the marks of two bullets in Jet's body—the one along his skull and another in the middle of his back.

It wasn't a good way to die—not for a fighting man.

The knowledge lay heavy and solid in Ben's mind. It didn't matter that Chico or Morrell had done the actual shooting. John Matson had been behind it, smooth and smiling and safe. He'd branded Jet with the name of murderer and spread the lie about his hanging. And there wasn't any law in Red Peak that would touch him.

Ben's eyes were cold and his jaw set hard as he slid Jet's gun from its holster and checked the load and got the feel of the gun in his hand. With a sudden shock of realization he knew that it was the same make and model as the one he'd given the boy when he was sixteen years old. Why hadn't he noticed that before? He'd been shunning his own share of the guilt.

He stared at the gun. This wasn't his way. It went against the hard-won truce he'd made with the violence that had once burned fierce and hot in him. He slid the gun back into its case.

Grimly he picked up the wide gun belt and buckled it around his middle. The gun lay heavy against his thigh. Two lengths of leather thong dangled from the end of the holster. Ben tied them above his knee, making the holster hug his leg tight and low. Now the gun seemed almost part of him.

Jet's way, but there was no other. Nancy's words would have a different meaning now. It was Jet who would face Matson for the final reckoning. Ben would only be the finger on the trigger.

Twenty-One

There was little chance of getting close to Matson through the front doors and past his barrier of hired guns. Ben studied the back of the saloon for several minutes. He'd worked his way along the foot of the cliff behind the row of buildings. Just as he had figured, the sentry on Red Peak had been pulled off long before. By now Ben was supposed to be dead. Matson would be relaxed and unworried, waiting for Julie to return with the news.

There was a back door and a window with curtains drawn. Overhead a narrow balcony ran across the rear of the saloon. Several windows led off the balcony, all dark. Sounds of loud talk and the tinny rhythm of the piano came muffled to Ben from inside the building. He speculated about his chances of plunging in fast through the back door and catching Matson by surprise, but he saw that this way would lean too much on luck. A bullet could cut him down before his eyes had a chance to pick Matson out from the crowd.

He peered up again at the balcony. One of the windows now showed a pale light. Ben was pretty sure what he'd find behind those windows. There was risk here, too, but at least there wouldn't be a whole company of Matson's gunslingers in his way.

Several horses were tethered beneath the balcony. Ben slipped close to the building and moved over to the horses. One shied nervously, and Ben clucked in a soothing way. He waited till they settled down before pushing against the flank of the end horse to make him swing in closer under the balcony. Carefully Ben swung up into the saddle. He could reach a supporting post of the balcony and he used it for balance as he stood erect in the stirrups and brought first one foot, then the other, up to the saddle. Standing on the horse this way he was able to reach the balcony railing.

As he started to draw himself up the horse skittered out from under him. Ben's grip on the railing with his good right hand held, but he hung suspended, legs dangling, lacking the strength to pull himself up with one arm. Setting his teeth against the sudden, searing pain, Ben caught the railing with his broken left hand and slowly, painfully hauled himself up. One of the horses whinnied softly.

He tumbled over the railing onto the balcony just as the rear door of the saloon opened below him. A bar of yellow light slashed out from the building, framing a man's shadow. Ben lay still. He was breathing hard and the pain slid up his arm in waves as hot as toothache. Feet scuffed the ground below.

"What's the matter, boy?" a voice spoke. "You hear somethin'?"

Ben was grateful the horse couldn't talk. For a long

minute the man stood silently under the balcony. Then he gave a grunt. His footsteps scraped dirt. The door opened again, letting loose its flood of sound, and shut. Once more the night was quiet.

Nearby a woman giggled. Ben waited. Finally he wormed his way on his belly until he was next to the wall of the building beneath a window ledge. He heard more smothered laughter and a man's hoarse whisper. Cautiously he crawled along to the next window. It was here that a light showed behind drawn curtains. The window was partly open, and he heard clearly the labored sounds of activity. Frowning, Ben continued along the balcony until he was under the last window. It was partly open and the room was dark. There was no sound. He waited a moment, then put his hand under the edge of the window to push up.

A voice spoke almost in his ear. "Come on, let's go."

"Aw, honey, I'm tired," a man mumbled.

Ben sank down. It was a busy night in Matson's place.

"Well, you can't sleep here," the woman said impatiently. "Come on, you've had your turn."

The man grumbled protestingly, but a moment later there came the noise of creaking springs and then his stumbling progress across the room. A match was struck and a lamp flickered and grew steady, turned down low. Then a door opened.

"Can't we jest—"

"No," the woman said, cutting him off.

The door closed and the room was silent. Ben eased the window open quickly and clambered through it. He slipped past the bed and a washstand and over to the door. As he drew his gun the door burst open without warning. Ben jumped to the side.

"Here we are, Joe!" a woman said cheerfully. "Just like home sweet home."

"Ya wouldn't kid me, would ya, Bess?"

Ben had a glimpse of a bare-shouldered woman in a flaming red dress and a cowboy who lurched unsteadily as the two stepped past him into the room. He shut the door quickly behind them. The woman whirled.

"Hey, what is this?" she cried.

"Don't yell," Ben snapped.

"Huh?" the cowboy gaped at him. "Who are you? Bess, I thought you said—"

Ben laid the barrel of the gun across the cowboy's skull, not too hard. He sank to the floor with a soft and secret sigh. The woman started to scream, and Ben wrapped his left arm over her face, muzzling her. For a moment she struggled. Ben let her feel the cold steel of his gun against her neck. She stiffened and was still.

"You just do what I say and you won't get hurt," Ben said softly.

He took his arm away from her mouth. She backed away from him, frightened.

"What is this?" she whispered, her voice trembling. "What do you want? Listen, you don't have to pull a gun on me. If you want to—"

"Shut up!" Ben made his voice rough. "I'm not here for fun. All you have to do is listen."

The man on the floor groaned.

"You hurt Joe," the woman whimpered. "What do you want of me? I don't know you."

"I'll tell you," Ben said. His voice was low but harsh with

command. "I want you to call one of the other girls over to the door. Don't let her in, just tell her to go get Matson. You can say the cowboy here is sick bad and there might be trouble. You don't know what to do with him. Tell her it has to be Matson, you understand?"

"Yeah, but I don't get it. He's just downstairs. Why can't you—" She gasped. "You—you're Webber! That's who you are!"

"Never mind who I am," Ben said. "Do what I say!"

"I—I can't! Matson'd kill me!"

"Maybe," Ben said grimly. "But maybe is better than sure."

Hating what he had to do, he prodded her with the gun threateningly. She gave a frightened little cry and backed hastily toward the door.

"I'll be right behind you," Ben warned. "And I'll be listening close. Say just what I told you."

Thoroughly scared now, the woman did what she was told. Ben stood beside her, concealed behind the door, while she called to another girl and repeated Ben's words.

"Dammit, Bess, I'm busy!" the girl complained. "Why can't you go yourself?"

"I can't leave him!" Bess pleaded tearfully. "Hurry!"

"Oh, all right!"

Ben pushed the door almost closed, leaving a crack.

"That's fine," he whispered. "Now back in the corner. And don't you make a sound, you hear?"

She shrank back. There was silence then except for her faint, terrified whimpering. Ben wondered if the ruse would work. If Matson sent one of his hands, there was no chance that Ben could get past him and still catch Matson by surprise. He was counting on Matson riding close herd on any trouble in his own saloon.

It seemed a long time before Ben heard the heavy clump of boots approaching. He tensed. The door pushed open.

"Bess? What the hell is—"

Matson saw Ben. His shoulder dropped as his right hand dipped toward his gun.

"Try it!" Ben snapped.

Matson froze with his hand on his gun. Very carefully he let his hand drop away.

"That's just fine," Ben said. He eyed Matson coldly, wishing that he could pull the trigger now when it was sure. But that kind of killing wasn't in him.

"Now back out slow," Ben said.

Matson backed onto the balcony overlooking the big main room of the saloon. Ben crowded him.

"Turn around," he ordered.

When Matson obeyed Ben stepped forward quickly and slipped the gun from Matson's holster. He shoved it under his own belt. He had to use his left hand to do it but he was oblivious of the pain.

"Now walk down the steps, slow and easy," Ben said. "And if one of your boys makes a move, you get it first."

Cursing in a low, savage voice, Matson walked along the balcony and started down the stairs, Ben close behind him. They were halfway down before anyone noticed what was happening.

"Hey, look!" a man shouted.

There was a confusion of movement and voices. "It's Webber." "Webber." "He's got a gun."

"Hold it!" Matson called out, panic giving an edge to the

sharp command in his voice. "He's got the drop on me!"

The room was very silent then. They reached the bottom of the stairs. Ben rammed his gun into Matson's back, prodding him forward. The crowd near the bar gave way before them, making an aisle. Passing some of Matson's narrow-eyed gunslicks, Ben felt his scalp prickling as if with heat.

"We'll take that table over there," Ben ordered.

The table was in the rear of the room and over to the side. Ben circled to the chair which had its back to the wall. He motioned Matson into the seat directly across from him. Ben let himself down into his chair carefully, keeping his gun trained on Matson's middle just above his belt. Matson was sweating.

"Seems to me I remember we was havin' a drink together," Ben said softly. "Let's have a bottle."

Matson licked his lips, hesitating, unsure of himself. Then he jerked his head toward the bar. "A bottle!" he said harshly. "You heard him!"

The bartender brought over a fresh bottle and two glasses. He set them gingerly on the table near the edge and quickly withdrew. Out of the corner of his eye Ben saw a lean figure edging to the side.

"One of your boys figures he'd like to see you die," Ben said. Deliberately he thumbed back the hammer of his gun. "As sure as he draws on me, you'll get a bullet in the belly."

"Don't try anything!" Matson called sharply, fear pulsating in his throat.

"Tell him to move out where I can see him," Ben commanded.

After a moment the lean gunman sidled over behind

Matson. Ben recognized the man who'd followed him out of the restaurant, the one he'd knocked out and tied up. Hate glittered in his eyes.

"He might be overanxious," Ben said softly to Matson. "Have him take off his gun belt and drop it, nice and careful."

The sweat was running down Matson's forehead. He'd lost his well-groomed, polished look. "Do what he says!" he snapped.

The gun belt thumped on the floor. Someone coughed, and the sound was a small explosion in the taut silence.

Ben nodded toward the bottle. "You do the pourin'," he said. "You're good at that, as I recall."

He paused, waiting until Matson began to pour. Then with his left hand he worked Matson's gun loose from his waist and carefully slid it across the table until it was right in front of Matson.

"When the bottle's empty," Ben said slowly, "I'll be puttin' my gun on the table. Then you can make your move."

There was a murmur from the watching crowd, the excited whisper of voices picking up Ben's words and repeating them. Ben saw the quick leap of hope in Matson's eyes and the attempt to shut it out so it wouldn't show.

"That's more chance than you gave my boy," Ben said.

Matson pushed one of the full glasses across to Ben. His hand was steady now. "I don't know what you're talkin' about," he said. Confidence was returning to him visibly, and he even managed a thin, contemptuous smile as he reached for his own glass.

"Keep both your hands above the table," Ben said. "And pick up the glass in your right hand."

Because he was holding the gun in his own right hand, Ben had to use his left to pick up his glass. The hand was stiff and swollen now, puffy red across the knuckles. Ben made a kind of awkward fist around his glass and managed to pick it up. He waited until Matson's throat worked in swallowing before he drank himself. He drained the glass. Matson eyed him speculatively and finished his drink.

"Pour," Ben said.

There was more talk now throughout the room. Ben could hear quick exchanges. Someone quoted odds, another answered him. They were betting on the outcome. He smiled thinly. He doubted if much money would be riding on him to win.

Matson refilled the glasses. Ben could see his mind working. He would be remembering how easily he had got Ben drunk the night before. Having the guns on the table instead of in holsters took away some of the advantage of a man with a fast draw, but Matson would still figure himself as the quicker—and steadier. Amusement began to play around his lips. He raised his glass.

"To fair play," he said with a sneer, and drank. "You overplayed your hand, Webber. You should have shot me when you had the chance—or you ought to do it right now—but you couldn't do that, could you? That's too bad, because I'm going to kill you."

Ben said nothing. He wanted Matson to start talking. The whisky was beginning to loosen his tongue.

"Now your boy Jet was different. He'd have killed me without blinkin' an eye. He didn't have your . . . sense of honor. He wasn't above shootin' a man without givin' him a chance."

The words broke through Ben's enforced calm. "If you mean Pardee," he said, "Jet didn't kill him."

Matson smiled. "The town knows different. That's why he was hanged, Webber. Bein' his father you naturally won't—"

"He wasn't hanged," Ben said.

The flat statement startled Matson and shook him. He looked around uneasily. Everyone was listening now. "That's crazy," Matson said. "Everyone knows—"

"I found his grave," Ben said. "He was shot twice. From the back."

Matson licked his lips nervously. Ben could see the other questions crowding into his mind: How had Ben escaped the trap set for him? Where were Red and Chico? What had happened to Julie? How much did Ben know? Ben let him sweat a little more.

"All right," Matson said suddenly. "I wouldn't know anythin' about it, but suppose he wasn't hanged. The posse shot him, that's all. You can't blame them for sayin' they hanged him."

"There was no posse."

"You're loco! You can say all you want, but nothin' will change the fact that your son was seen to shoot Pardee down in cold blood."

"I was wonderin' about that," Ben said evenly. "I reckon that was the cleverest part of all you did, because folks trusted Indian Joe. How did you get him to say he saw the shootin'? Did he just hear the shots and think he saw Jet— maybe with a little help? Or did you stage a little show for him, so's you'd have a witness to somethin' that never happened?"

The guess struck home. "You're just talkin' wild!" Matson retorted angrily. But he was flustered. He poured the glasses full once more, but this time the whisky slopped over, spilling onto the table. His hand wasn't quite so sure. The bottle showed less than half full.

"I reckon you had it acted out for him," Ben mused speculatively. "You had somebody wear black clothes like Jet's—Chico, maybe. He was the same size. And Joe couldn't see the difference. Then later you had him dig the grave, not lettin' him see the body close to, tellin' him the boy had been hanged. He'd have no reason to disbelieve it."

Matson laughed harshly. "You pick a good witness, Webber—a man who's dead and can't call your hand."

"That's right," Ben said softly. "He had to die. He knew where the body was buried. You bribed him not to say, and he didn't think it mattered at first. Then when you got scared that he might tell me, you had him killed."

"I don't have to listen to this!" Matson snarled.

"You'll listen!" Ben's voice was cold and deadly. "The town will listen. Your Julie has already done a heap of talkin'."

"Julie!" Matson's lips were white with rage. "What have you done to her?"

"She'll keep," Ben said. He'd emptied his glass. The whisky burned in his belly but his mind was cold with an anger beyond any surface heat, as cold and hard and lethal as the gun pointing at Matson's chest. But he knew he couldn't hold the icy calm much longer. "You're not drinkin'," he said pointedly.

For a moment longer the hate raged uncontrolled in Matson's face. Then abruptly it withdrew. The arrogant contempt returned, as if he had just remembered that it didn't really matter what Ben knew or what the town believed. He was big enough and powerful enough to ride herd on all of Red Peak regardless. All he had to do was kill Ben. After that, if he thought it necessary, it would be easy enough to give the lie to the charges Ben had made. There was no real proof.

He tossed down his drink. His hand seemed steadier again as he filled the glasses. With a little smile he held up the bottle to the light. "One more," he said.

Together they held up the glasses and drank. When Matson put his down, his cheeks were flushed and his eyes bright. Ben drank more slowly, and Matson made a show of waiting for him to finish. Then, very carefully, he emptied the bottle, measuring each glass to an equal amount.

"You said an even chance," Matson said, eyeing Ben's gun.

"I did."

Ben stared at him across the table. He wondered why he had done it this way. What was he trying to prove? He should have had no compunctions about shooting Matson on sight, any more than he'd hesitate to shoot any crawling sidewinder. Was it because of the beating he'd taken the night before when Matson had got him drunk? Or was he trying to prove to himself that he could sit at a table across from Matson with a gun in his hand and not pull the trigger? The gun itself might be the reason. Jet's gun. He had to use it fair and clean.

Ben didn't allow himself to look around the room or to think about what Matson's men would do now, and whether the ranchers would have the courage to side with him if Matson's gunslingers jumped in.

"You're a sidewindin' killer," Ben said quietly into the room's tense stillness. "You don't deserve dyin' easy with a bullet. If I'd thought you'd hang for what you done, I might have been satisfied with that. But I can't be sure you wouldn't wiggle out of it."

"You tryin' to back down?" Matson sneered. "You'll never leave this room alive, Webber. You can't crawl out now."

Ben waited for Matson to pick up his glass. Then, very deliberately, Ben set his gun on the table and took his own glass in his right hand.

"For Jet," Ben said, and he drank.

Too late he saw that Matson hadn't waited to drink. Matson dropped his glass and rose in one smooth motion, and his gun hand moved with blinding speed—not toward the gun on the table but to another holster Ben hadn't seen under his left armpit. The hand slashed under and reappeared too fast for the eye to follow it. Ben grabbed for his gun and pitched to the side off his chair in a hasty, clumsy movement. He saw the round black hole of Matson's gun muzzle spit orange flame.

Maybe Matson's aim had been dulled by drink or thrown off by his frantic speed. Maybe the pressure built up by the long wait had played too much on his nerves and undermined his sureness. Maybe it was fear, in a gambler who didn't like the odds too even. Or maybe it was just that Matson hadn't counted on Ben's pitch to the side and he'd fired at the spot where Ben should have been. The shot missed. Falling, Ben brought his own gun level as Matson's second quick shot tugged at his shirt. He fired from the floor. The gun kicked in his hand and kicked again and Matson straightened up high on his toes, shocked disbelief frozen on his face, his hand clutching automatically at the holes that opened up in his chest. Ben's finger kept on squeezing without any volition of his own. Matson lurched forward into the third bullet, which split his forehead. His body jerked and toppled, slow at first, then faster, bouncing off a table and smacking the floor with an ugly thump.

Ben was only dimly aware of the burst of gunfire around him and the shouting. It shut off suddenly and there was a moment's eerie silence, broken by a moan and a woman's whimper. Out of the corner of his eye Ben saw the lean gunman kneeling on the floor where his hand still reached for the gun he'd been forced to drop. He was coughing blood.

Then talk burst forth, a confusion of orders and curses. Ben saw Zeke Lucas with a smoking gun. Along the bar several of Matson's men had raised their hands. He knew then that the ranchers had backed him in time.

Twenty-two

Order came quickly. Matson's men were lined along the wall and disarmed. Ben thought they'd soon be riding out of Red Peak—fast. One, the lean gunman, was dying from a bullet Lucas had fired, and another was wounded. Only one of the ranchers had been nicked in the firing. Their leader dead, Matson's men hadn't been too eager for the battle.

Ben started toward the door. He passed a grinning cowboy collecting his winnings.

"You lemme know next time you're in a fight," the cowboy called.

"There'll be no next time," Ben said.

Julie Larkin burst through the swinging doors and rushed past him. Seconds later her scream cut through the pall of gunsmoke. Ben felt a twist of pity.

Nancy was waiting just outside the doors. Ben stopped, and they looked at each other without speaking. Her eyes started to shine unnaturally, and tears trickled silently down her cheeks. She turned her head away.

"I heard you won," she said.

Ben nodded. "It's over," he said.

"Dammit, you always see me cryin'!" she cried. "I don't usually. Not much, anyways."

"I'm not complainin'."

She lifted her face and saw him grinning down at her. She blinked and an uncertain smile broke through her tears. Ben thought of spring blooming, and his heart lifted. She was as pretty as a mountain valley after an early rain, fresh and moist and glittering in the new sun.

"The sheriff's on his way here," she said irrelevantly. "One of the boys found him."

"I figured he'd show up soon now."

"We put Morrell in jail. He's the one that shot Ross." She spoke quietly, without bitterness. "He'll hang for it. It was Chico who shot Jet."

Men were pushing out of the saloon, crowding around

183

them. Ben took Nancy's arm and guided her out of the way. They walked slowly down the boardwalk. He kept his hand on her arm, liking the warmth and strength he felt in her.

"Your job's done here," she said abruptly. "You'll be takin' Jet home."

"Yep." He halted and turned her around to face him. "You'll be stayin' here in town?"

"I reckon," she said soberly. "Till it's straightened out about the ranch."

"I'll be back," Ben said. "I was hopin' you'd be here."

Suddenly she smiled. "You'll be welcome, Ben."

Center Point Publishing
600 Brooks Road • PO Box 1
Thorndike ME 04986-0001 USA

(207) 568-3717

US & Canada:
1 800 929-9108